The Cincinnati Kid

The Cincinnati Kid

A NOVEL BY

RICHARD JESSUP

Little, Brown and Company · Boston · Toronto

To my very good friend

JAY SANFORD

The Cincinnati Kid

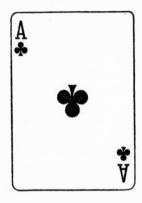

He was a skinny kid, just twenty-six when it started, with a face set off by a large nose that gave him the look of a hawk. He was a tight man. Everything about him was close and quiet; his gestures were short and clean, with no wasted movement. His eyes were bright and hard, the kind of blue you might see in the sky at high noon, if you looked straight up at the sky; almost white, but still pale, pale blue. He had dark yellowish circles under his eyes that rested on his cheekbones where the skin was drawn tight, as if he might have liver trouble from too much drinking, but he was physically sound and the circles came from playing stud poker all day and all night for many years.

He had been playing in the back room of Hoban's Pool Room and Poker Parlor since Monday at 4 P.M.

It had started out as fooling around and then, as happened so many times, it developed into a game. The others began to drop in and a gig was working. It was nickel-and-dime stuff as long as it was The Kid and The Shooter and Pig, but when Carey and Carmody came in, both of whom bet the Cardinals and had won nicely over the weekend double-header, the play moved, deceptively, from nickel-and-dime to a quarter and a half and then wide open.

It was Wednesday now, eleven in the morning. The game, like an endlessly circling bird, moved with a slow inexorable pace toward the center pot of money that grew magically with each dealt hand; revolving hands of cards, accompanied with a musical comment of silver upon silver tossed into the center of the table as the chant was heard, so soft as to be a litany calling on ghostly assistance and deliverance.

"Queens bet."

"A half."

"In."

"Kicking it a half."

"And another half."

"And a half more."

"Buck and a half to me, and a half more."

The ritual quickened. It was the fourth card. Now the whisper and flutter of paper money would wash into the middle of the table.

Someone dealt. The cards sliced through the

smoky airless room like silent stealing death. And with each card, face up, a chant of destiny from the dealer, for he was the sole instrument in the life of a rambling-gambling man, bringing face up for all the world to see the next wonderful secret. There is nothing more for the gambling man. It is all there, sealed in the narrow turn of the next card.

"A five to the queens, a jack to the possible, a nothing to the fours, an ace to the kicker, and the Gun shoots himself a red ten. Still queens."

"Queens check."

The raiser came back with a touch, a breath, feeling his way into those checking queens like a man fumbling in the dark. He touched it and then the queens slammed down hard on him.

"Twenty dollars."

It was the clap of doom. Three players dropped out and it was back to the raiser. He hesitated. He knew three fours could not beat three queens. And to make sure (though there was another card coming and another chance) there were three queens, it would cost him twenty dollars. Pig had the fours. The Kid had the queens.

They looked at each other's cards. They were past the point as rambling-gambling men where they could play each other's faces. Pig played the cards. There was no hope in playing The Kid. And it was not worth twenty dollars to see if The Kid was bluffing. He folded.

The Shooter gathered up the cards and began to shuffle. In his huge hands the cards were like summer moths around a light, fluttering, singing, tightening and then disappearing as he cut them and rippled them again. The Shooter was acknowledged as the best man with cards along the Mississippi and west to Vegas. He looked over at The Kid who was stacking his half dollars. "They say Lancey is in town," he said softly.

The Kid turned his pale blue eyes on The Shooter. "Yeah?" he said slowly. "You don't say."

They all knew The Kid had been waiting, and that he had been restless lately. Pig, Carey and Carmody looked at their money. The Shooter looked at The Kid. But The Kid didn't say anything, and The Shooter had already taken the deal through the fourth shuffle and began to peel them off.

Hoban came in and made his collection. In the old fashioned poker parlors the pot is never cut for the house, instead the chairs are rented by the house to the player on an hourly basis. Hoban took fifteen cents from each player and worked on a jaw tooth with a toothpick, an idle fat man who never played poker for fear of losing and, watching a few hands, slouched back to the front of the pool room and stood in back of the cigar counter and watched Harold Street. About one o'clock the girl came in with coffee and sandwiches, and after taking a pair of good pots in a row, The Shooter stood up and an-

nounced he had had enough. They all waited for
The Kid to get up too, and he did.

Then they knew.

St. Louis was hot that spring. It is always hot in
summer, and this is to be expected, but not in the
spring. It was only a little while since the flood season, which is always cold and damp, and there it was,
a soaring ninety-five-degree heat in the middle of
May. At three o'clock on Harold Street it felt like
July; the kids were gasping for breath playing out
their sidewalk games, and old men sat on front steps
wriggling their yellowing toes and drinking beer,
while women hung out of the windows and called
back and forth to each other. It was unusually hot
for spring. Everybody said so. But where the heat
would do the most good, it had so far had little
effect. The Cardinals were getting off to a slow start.
Musial wasn't hitting. But then everybody knew that
he was a slow starter, and needed the true heat of
summer, day after day, to get him going. The Cardinals weren't going anyplace until he was right.

Harold Street was not too far from the river. It
was the last street in St. Louis to have streetcar
tracks still in the ground, though the streetcars themselves had vanished long ago. Uptown streets were
blacked over and smooth and slick from curb to
curb; the uptown tracks had been taken up and
used, some said, as supports for the levee on the

lower river. But there on Harold Street, the cobble-stones were still in the ground and the tracks were filled in with dirt and grime, and when it rained, old trucks with slick tires would get caught in the tracks and slide as much as ten feet. This happened usually when the trucks tried to make the turn into Broom Street. Romany Gypsies, Arkansas farmers, Memphis Negroes, and Missouri White Trash, lived there, with a few Jews and Irishers, and they were all third- and fourth-generation families who had lived near the river, and had been dominated by the river and who had never lived anyplace else and did not want to live anyplace else.

There was not much more to Harold Street than you could see; several blocks of stores and cheap hotels and rooming houses and upstairs apartments; a drugstore, a five-and-dime, an A&P, several fruit-stands, an Army-Navy Store and a pawnshop with the usual brass knucks, mottled nickel-plated pistols and hunting knives; there was a Catholic Church and a Baptist Church, and then you were either mov-ing into the uptown area, away from the river, or you were on the old wooden pier and the river it-self. They still swam in the river in the summer, and they fished and drank and brawled and moved from day to day and did not question or think about their lives, or anything, except what they might think when it was dark and quiet in the middle of the night when he rolled over and reached for her, or when she had to get up and see about the children.

The Kid and The Shooter walked up Harold Street toward the Mills Hotel where the big man stayed when he was down and close to the edge of his stake. The hotel got a big play since it was only two buildings away from the river itself and the view from the upper rooms was a very good one of the river. The Shooter had been living on the edge for a long time now. Some said it was because he was getting old and losing interest, but The Kid did not believe the talk. He sensed rather than knew that The Shooter was just not pushing as hard any more; The Shooter was in a vacuum and he knew it and knew that it would break of its own accord and he did not try to break it himself.

They stood together on the pier and looked at the river and watched the working boats of the Army Engineers who were always taking some kind of survey; this day they were setting up ranges in the river, red and white diamonds.

"Yeah, I been seeing it come for a long time, Kid," The Shooter said, lighting a cigar and looking around the river and back up the bright sunlighted street, and wincing against the light. "Long time."

"Yeah," The Kid said, nodding his head. "Yeah, I guess maybe you could, Shooter. I ain't exactly been hiding it under a bushel basket."

"No, you ain't been hiding it." The Shooter said. "That's something going for you."

The Kid didn't say anything.

"But Lancey's close to death," The Shooter said.

"Well," The Kid said. "I gotta know."

"Sure you gotta know," The Shooter said sympathetically. "That's what made me tell you he's around."

"What?"

"We all gotta know," The Shooter said. "Sometime or other, we gotta find out how much juice we got."

"You ever sit down with him?"

"Yes," The Shooter said, "I have."

The Kid waited. The Shooter pursed his lips and looked up and down Harold Street and then out to the river.

"Well, what happened?" The Kid asked impatiently.

"Why, nothing, Kid. Nothing at all."

"You lost."

"No, I dint lose. I'm too good to lose when I set my mind to it. I play poker a certain way, Kid. I been where I'm going, know what I mean?"

"No, I don't follow you."

"I've had my Lancey Hodges. Only with me, it was Whistling Sam Magee to New Orleans."

"I heard about him," The Kid said respectfully.

"Well, then you know it all. About thirty years

ago, I guess, maybe more. It was me and Whistling Sam. He was my Lancey Hodges."

"What happened?"

The Shooter looked at The Kid with mild surprise in his eye and in his voice. "Why, I lost it, Kid. It dried me up on the inside for a long, a very long time."

"Yeh?" The Kid said, interested.

But the Shooter didn't elaborate. The Kid nodded, looked out over the river and watched the work boats of the engineers, twin red castles on a buff yellow field painted on the stern and bow of the boats as familiar to people who knew the river as the mudcat fishermen's skiffs. When he came out of his thoughts, he looked up at The Shooter who stood as patient as Job, smoking a two-dollar cigar and studying the middle distance.

"You think I'm ready?" The Kid asked.

The Shooter didn't answer for a long time. He took time to puff the cigar several times and the answer was slow in coming. "Kid, I don't think you're ready."

"Oh," The Kid said quickly, not expecting this kind of honesty, but after thinking about it, realized that The Shooter, who never had a bad word to say about anyone, and who never had a bad word said about him, would not con him.

"But you're not going to take my word for it, are you?" The Shooter said. "Are you now?"

"No," The Kid said stubbornly. "I ain't. I can't."

The Shooter nodded his head several times, as if he had known. "I know, I know," he said quietly, respectfully. "You got to find out for yourself. See? That's why I told you he was in town. He's right here, right now, on the river, now. Over to the Washburn Hotel in a game right this minute."

"I don't figure to take him right away," The Kid said, "but if I can hang in there long enough, I can outlast him. If I can outlast him, I got a chance. You admit that, don't you, that I got a chance?"

"I awready said that I dint think you were ready," The Shooter said.

"Did you think you were ready when you sat down with Whistling Sam Magee?"

"Kid, I thought I was the best poker player in the world," The Shooter said and had taken the time to remove the cigar again and face The Kid when he spoke. "I'm telling you now, I thought I was the *best*."

"Well, I don't think I'm just a cocky square with a fair hand with cards," The Kid said defensively. "I got something."

"No, you ain't no cocky square," The Shooter said mildly. "An' you probly got something."

"Okay," The Kid said and looked out over the river. "And I ain't saying that you was either, when you sat down with Whistling Sam."

"I know what you mean, Kid," The Shooter said

easily. "Don't you know now, that an old bull like me can smell, I mean, as long as I been on the river, that I can't feel out a case of nerves in a lunsman? But don't discount cock in a man, Kid. It can give a very fair and middle-class man a good ride. Cock in a man will carry. I remember them Cardinals. Ol' Pepper stealing everything in sight, an' ol Leo acting like he was a real lion. Two-fifty hitters but four hundred in cock. I seen guys in my time with nothin', jest nothin' and they take stiffener into a game with 'em and they made out good. It ain't wise to carry cock with you all the time, cause it takes the edge off the real stuff. But if you *got* the stuff, being a little sassy don't hurt you none. See what I mean?"

The two men looked at each other.

"Well," The Kid said doggedly, "would you say if I got any chance at all?"

"This much of a chance," The Shooter said. "If Lancey is not right. If he's got a cold, or his stomach ulcer is acting up, or something like that. But then it won't prove anything. You can see that. It won't prove a thing, because everybody'll see he's not right." The Shooter thought a moment, nodded his head and put the cigar back in his mouth and chewed the end contentedly, and, with the satisfaction of a man who knows he is not going to be hustled into any challenges, he studied the river.

The Kid's face clouded over stubbornly. "So!" he said with a mild explosive blow through his lips.

♠ 13

"There ain't but one thing to do and that's find out."

"Then you made up your mind?" The Shooter asked, really interested now that The Kid, obviously, was determined to sit down with Lancey Hodges.

"I gotta. You said that yourself, that I gotta," The Kid said with a bite to his tone. "I'm overdue for it as it is."

"Yeah, you been around a long time," The Shooter said. "I was a lot younger than you when I went up against Whistling Sam." The Shooter looked at The Kid speculatively. "But you'd be kinda young, too, to be The Man."

"I gotta find out," The Kid said and turned away quickly, but not before The Shooter saw a painful stitch cross the younger man's face.

"Want me to see to it?"

The Kid looked up gratefully. "I wish you would, Shooter Man."

"All right, I'll do it. I'll set it up with Lancey, and spread the word."

"What word?"

"You gotta look at this thing a certain way, Kid," The Shooter said. "There's all sorts of rambling-gambling men want to sit down with Lancey, and he can't take them all on, all the time. It's got to be a serious thing. But once someone in my class spreads the word, and it's legit, then regardless what Lancey feels like, he's gotta take you on. See what I mean?"

The Kid nodded.

"I'll let him know you want to sit down."

"One thing, Shooter," The Kid said with a worried look on his face.

"What?"

"About spreading the word. Lancey might not think I'm up to him. And turn me down. I wouldn't want it known, if he doesn't think I'm high enough for him to try on."

"Kid, if Lancey turned you down, you'd *be* The Man. He's got to take you on. Somebody in your class? Sure, what you think? And man, I'm here to tell you, he knows you're around. He can probably smell meat like you a mile and a half up the river. He knows you're around, and he'll sit down with you. I can garntee it, if you want me to, by telling Big Nig right away. You want to butt heads with The Man, I'll set it up. I'll be in touch," The Shooter said, then nodded his head at a honey blonde a half block away. "Here comes your woman."

"Okay, then, you'll set it up. You won't forget now?"

"I done tol' you, Kid, I'd see to it. Go get some sleep. Plenty of sleep and forget about cards. It won't be for at least a week."

"Why so long?" The Kid asked. "I wouldn't want to sit around too long. I want to get in and get it over with."

"Lancey's got a big game going, I hear. Got some

♠ 15

pretty fair country poker players with loot to burn — Texas oil, I heard — over to the Washburn. I can't ask a man to let go of an easy dollar like that. Then he's gotta have some time to rest up for you. You wouldn't wanta take him on when he wasn't right."

"Oh," The Kid said. "Oh, well, if he's tooling a dollar, I can unnerstand that. Sure."

"Not earlier than a week," The Shooter said. "But not much more than that either."

"A week," The Kid said.

"Eat a lot of greens and red meat and drink milk. Eat and rest and play with your woman. And go down to the Y and work out a little. Take steam baths. Get yourself into shape." The Shooter tapped The Kid's stomach lightly, assuming a boxing pose for a brief moment. "Maybe get outa town for a day or two and breathe some fresh air. It ain't going to be easy on you."

The Kid tightened. "How's it going to be?"

"Kid, you're going in there with a killer and he's got a lot to protect."

"Like what?"

"He's The Man, see? And all the squares that play cards know he's The Man and invite him to sit in on their little square games and lose to him, jus' so they can say they played with him, see? So, I mean, Kid, he's got a lot to protect. Right now, over to the Washburn, with that Texas money. He'll come away with a roll. But they wouldn't let you or me in the

16 ♠

game. He's a celebrity. He's got a lot to protect, and he'll suck you in and kill you off quick as he can to maybe throw a scare in another comer like you up the line somewhere that you and me ain't never heard of yet, but who knows about Lancey as The Man, see what I mean?"

"Yeh," The Kid said, a little stubbornly, looking at his woman as she approached.

"He'll use everything in the book, an' then some he's made up," The Shooter said. "And once you go in, Kid, you can't quit. You get that straight right now. Two of you go in and only one of you can come out, 'cause there ain't room for two at the top, see it?"

The Shooter put his cigar back into his lips and puffed several times, studying the river. He started to remove the cigar and speak again, then he closed his mouth tight. He spoke around the long dark stem of tobacco. "Never mind. Just do like I tol' you to do. And don't drink."

The Kid listened to this advice and nodded his head.

"You got much of a stake?"

"Maybe eleven-twelve hundred," The Kid replied. And then asked quietly, "Will that be enough?"

"More than enough. A grand will give you a good ride and even if you don't win, why you'll come away with a good idea of what you're made out of."

"Well," The Kid said, "school's out. I damn sure don't want no lessons. I want everything he's got."

"It's the only way to be, Kid. See you." The Shooter turned away abruptly as the woman walked up.

The Kid nodded to the woman and turned to watch The Shooter going on down to the Mills Hotel, a big man with a heavy gut and a lazy, slow, lumbering way that hid the razor-sharp keenness of his mind, and then The Kid looked away, taking the woman by the arm, and crossed over Harold Street to Broom Street where they had two rooms over a grocery store.

Children growing up in the bottoms at the very edge of the Ohio River in Cincinnati, living in the old German-built, gray and brown and white clapboard houses three stories high and trimmed with gingerbread wood lace, learned to deal a deck of cards before they were out of grammar school. Rattling around the twenty-five-mile shoreline of the river, playing hide-and-seek and hitching rides on barges, exploring empty lofts and the tops of wholesale warehouses, tumbling in vacant lots next to manufacturing blocks, The Kid was lost to school when he was twelve and at thirteen was running a blackjack game for the Negro warehousemen on their lunch hour.

From thirteen to sixteen he began to *feel* the cards. They became more than just instruments of making money for the movies or a new pair of shoes, which was a very common device used by all of his friends. Out of these quiet, very desperate little penny games in alleys and on the decks of abandoned barges, on wintry street corners, the raw shoeshine boys' poker began to grow and he began to grow with it and when he had grown old enough, he began to hope there was a way open for him; and once he had discovered his feel for cards was real and genuine, an urgency began to rise in him and gain strength.

Out of those volatile games of poker The Kid gleaned by misplay and nerving experience the differences between winning and losing certain basic fundamentals that aid in a winning hand of stud poker. From Jo-Jo, a hulking Negro newspaper route boy, he learned never to stay unless the cards he held, including his hole card, could beat the board; from a bargeman, painfully losing his stake of twenty-seven dollars, he learned never to stay against an open pair, unless he could beat the pair or any possibility of a third card his opponent might have in the hole; from others he learned, sometimes by accident and luck, but mostly because he was growing and remembering every time he would lose, never to raise a pair unless the amount in the pot was at least five or six times the amount of the bet, including the raise; never to stay with two small pairs when there is a pair showing with extra cards higher than yours that can be paired with a hole card, or that can produce three of a kind. He learned about check and raise, and how to avoid it, and how to use it, and how and when to check a cinch; he learned how and when to buy a pot by betting ten and twenty times the amount in the pot; he learned about sticking to patterns of play that might lull his opponent into thinking he was going to stick to that pattern, and then reverse, only to have Bill O'Day spot his scheme and reverse on him and wipe him out. He learned other things too: never to win too much from a stranger who was bigger and stronger and could beat his tail and take all of the money. But this only happened once. The next time it was tried, he left the man half dead in an empty lot.

On his sixteenth birthday he started running himself ragged trying to figure out why there was a chance for him with cards and why it appealed to him; he made a serious effort to find out and it was not too long, because he really pressed this thing, before he discovered that a betting man with an honest dollar to back his judgment on a subject was equal to anyone, anywhere, any time, and that from time immemorial there had been men who would bet, rich men with poor, smart men with stupid men, black men with white men. The size of a man's bet was not a significant factor, nor what he bet on, nor how he bet. It was the idea of a man backing his judgment with something of value and taking the chance of losing. He took his pursuit further and discovered that businessmen were betting on their judgment, and young couples getting married were betting on their judgment, and that a stud game was the same thing, only it was a very narrow fraternity and did not contribute anything to society, or to the economy, or to the development of a town, or a man, or anything at all, except that it was a way for a man to go, and a way a man might have of making his way. He saw, accurately, that there was no difference between the stud man and the stocks and bonds man, and when he saw that he could dedicate his life to learning stocks and bonds, or real estate, and that it would still be his judgment he would be backing with a bet, he turned back to cards because he had been with cards for so long a time and had a head start. And then he recognized that he had this truly fine feeling for them.

On his seventeenth birthday he moved across the river to Kentucky and began learning the difference between playing cards and being a rambling-gambling man. It was still a question of a man backing his judgment and making his bet and winning or losing. But there was more subtlety in the mores and patterns of behavior amongst the professionals than he had ever known with just pick-up games. While he had been playing winning poker on his side of the river, it was strictly social poker and not professional at all. Professional card men, he saw, were really no different from any other card players except in their attitude. It was their whole life and nothing got in the way of it.

Moving into this life The Kid began to learn, first, the rules governing conduct of the rambling-gambling man with his fellows. The most outstanding characteristic The Kid soon discovered was their need for one another. It was never a problem for a rambling-gambling man to locate a game and sit down; it was something else again to find keen competition, honest competition of a standard and excellence of play that astounded The Kid when he first observed it, and touched it.

This need was demonstrated to The Kid in one of his first games across the East River (which is what card men called the Ohio River, with the Missouri being the West River, and the Mississippi called simply, The River) when one of the players had lost everything and made the general statement to the table that he was Tap City. All of the players present gave the loser several dollars, and when The Kid asked why, being a hardhead about money, he was told that Tap City money was for the rambling-gambling man to get on his feet again.

The Kid, moving into this quiet, all-night world of card men who could be found in any city along the banks of the three rivers, learned that card men never loaned money to each other. A man's stake had to be raised outside of the fraternity and sources of supply were the state secrets for each man.

Slowly, adding on, there in the poker parlors of Covington and Newport, Kentucky, in the hall bedroom games, in the kitchen games, moving from the garage games to hotel games, moving from the penny-and-three tables when he had built up his stake, to the nickel-and-dime action, he felt the difference in pressure and learned the difference in play as the stakes grew, from the quarter-and-a-half, to the one dollar no-limit. His resolve hardened, gained muscle, fleshed out, getting firm and strong; and then after several years of this, he began to gain poise with confidence that he might really have found a place for himself. In a little while, before he was twenty, he was to become The Cincinnati Kid.

He went through endless nights and long, long days of cards, and over the years, like many other natural card men, he soon dismissed blackjack as being a game of short bluff and limited scope. He tried faro, but there was not enough in it for him. He gave bridge a try, but didn't like the idea of partners. Once he settled into dominoes, but soon gave it up in raw disgust. He found a heady simplicity in craps, but still there was something in him that wanted a game where there was more personal control, and where it was he and he alone playing cards and not giving it all over to luck, or odds, as it was with horses and craps or roulette. So, finally, instinctively, The Kid gravitated to poker; first to draw poker and then he found stud to be the game that was right as rain.

By the time he was twenty-one, he was a full rambling-gambling man, a three-river man, which

was to say that he had been to and played in all of
the important places for a card man to play. From
Jolly's Omaha Card Club on the Missouri, to Spriigi's
Emporium in Wheeling on the Ohio, down to Big
Nig's in Memphis on the Mississippi, he was known
as The Cincinnati Kid, a comer, with a way about
him, and he was welcomed into any game from New
Orleans to the big steel payday games in Pittsburgh.

The Kid was on and off the edge of his stake many
times during his early build-up and schooling, and it
was noticed that he had begun to get flashy with his
card playing. It took Big Nig to teach The Kid a hard
lesson, when, as they were playing and The Kid had
been getting hot cards all night and betting everything strong, feeling that he could not miss, Big Nig
cooled him off with no-stay. Big Nig had sat there
and turned over seventy-three hands of cards before
he bet, and in that time, The Kid cooled off and Big
Nig took him. It was in a sense the last time The Kid
took a lesson and it straightened him out and he was
not so flashy any more, but quiet, and when he did
not crybaby about the way Big Nig had taken him,
it was forgotten and he was then fully accepted as a
member of the fraternity. Then he truly became a
three river man.

He had never gone east of Pittsburgh and for the
last few years had been using St. Louis as home base.
And it was during a game in East St. Louis in the
back of Victoria's Bar, with the game moving from

there to a St. Louis hotel and then out of the hotel to the drawing room of a millionaire candy manufacturer who was a good stud man and who did not want to break up the game just because he was on his way home to Cincinnati, that The Kid made his first trip back to the bottoms.

And this led him naturally across the river for a visit to the old haunts of Covington and Newport, where, out of action, he had seen Lancey Hodges, and the feeling had settled over him and he knew that Lancey was the man to play. There didn't seem to be any reason for it. It was just there.

Lancey Hodges was a thin man, short, with a banker's look about him, wearing a vest and an iron-gray summer suit, thin wispy hair brushed back over a gleaming skull, dead-white delicate fingers handling cards with the patience of a surgeon and with a surgeon's complete control and knowledge. His stake had been low or he would have sat down then.

Now he knew it was better that he hadn't. Lancey had only been a face to him, a rambling-gambling man who had drifted into the parlor of Miriam's kitchen game and was playing his cards. It did not take him long to learn who he was. This was Lancey Hodges. From Vegas to Brooklyn, Miami Beach to Covington, St. Louis to New Orleans, Lancey Hodges was The Man.

It was Miriam, a woman with a great talent for

scolding, and a bitterness about the way life had treated her that made her dippy on the subject of faith and promise, who told The Kid, in a flat, hard way, who Lancey was and what he represented.

"He come nice and clean into the world from a home to Savannah where everything's gotta be cleaned up and smoothed over, because that's the way things is been since they got there in town, with all that money and all, and all he's gotta do is jest sit on it and hold it and what's left of everything will make its way to him, and he don't care for nothing but diddling with cards. I knowed Lancey from back yonder. I see him to Nig's in Memphis and down to Yeller's in Noorlins, back yonder when they was shunting booze inta the country. Him. Sheet! Nothing but a comer like you, Kid, only he liked wimmen too. Always got to feel a leg, that's the kind he is. Oooeeeh! That sonsabitch is cold. I seen him gut a feller with a furth card and rattle him s'bad, the feller quit and got up and pissed red in the john and went square. They ain't but one way to ferk with the kind of man Lancey Hodges is, Kid, and that' to have a tree-mendous stake, and then sit there and wait fer his stomik to get him wild, then gut him. But you won't do nothin' with a little money. You got to be holding *wild* money. An' and I know you busted to the edge. But you growd some, Cincinnata. You kin make his stomik ulcer bleed, but I ain't got much faith in nothin' that will take him. He's liable to bleed to death right on a flush hand before he give up to you. He likes being The Man. But, now you looka here, at this here boy Lancey's sittin' with now, that nigger giving him a run, an ol' field hand up from Tennessee, ain't he got a way with cards? Well, this nigger will go down, but he's got some ride coming to him yit, so if you can raise your stake and get off'n the edge, you kin sit down with him, but you'll have to be quicker than three-four days. Lancey is going to gut this nigger. But I swear, Kid, I like to see that nigger make a deck move. Them hands is like flywheels on an old car. Makes me think of The Shooter, way he guns 'em out. Go on, Kid, you got time. Hustle somethin' and raise your load, and come on back."

But there was no time. Lancey reached the Negro field hand from Tennessee the next day and broke him and sent him out into the streets to shine shoes. And in that time, The Kid did something he had never done before and had never done since: he conned his way into a game in a first-class country club, not letting anyone know he was The Cincinnati Kid and a rambling-gambling man, and he got out of the game several thousand dollars clean. When he got back to Miriam's, Lancey had busted the field hand, who had refused Tap City money, which made the Negro stand high in the fraternity, and Lancey was gone, down to Big Nig's, Miriam said, and The Kid had gone after him.

"Don' mess 'round with The Man jest yit, Kid," Big Nig had warned him. "Jest learn a little mo' poker. Right now, Lancey'd take skin and leave you dried out like a sucked orange in the sun, juice all gone."

But it had worked on him. And after going on down to Yeller's in New Orleans and learning that Lancey had taken one of the cruise ships and was not in the country, The Kid stood on the levee and looked out over the river and for the first time in his life he began to think further than the hands of cards on the table in a game and he began to try to pierce the inner core of the science of playing stud poker. He had the art. The Shooter told him so when The Kid returned to St. Louis and described his feelings about Lancey to the big man.

"Kid," The Shooter had told him over beer in the Glassways Beer Garden that overlooked the river, "you're one of the truly great artists. Before you was twenty I heard about you even before you knew I was alive. Word comes fast on the three rivers when talent shows. It was all over about the Cincinnati Kid that was playing Miriam's and the parlors in Covey and Newport! Art! Whew! Man, you got the pure art. But you're going to need more than that if you sit down with Lancey Hodges. He's a dead eye, no nerves at all, and steel-minded, and Kid, *he knows.*"

The Kid lacked the depth and he was at a loss as to how he could change that. But he knew he had to.

It might have been that The Kid was a fast ball pitcher facing the home run hitter and lacked a curve ball to get him out of the inning. It might have been that The Kid was a natural welter and wondering if the extra pounds blowing him up to a middle weight would burden him. It might have been that The Kid was a brilliant designer of bridges and lacked the engineering. But he wasn't a fast ball pitcher, or a heavy welter, or a poor engineer. He was a three river man. A stud man. A member of the elite, and for him, Lancey Hodges was the way to go home free.

It didn't take long for the word to get around. They could all see that he was restless and they could see how he was experimenting. It was beyond protocol for them to ask why he was playing in such a probing way, but it didn't take long for them to find out, and they heard it all, his problems, his frustrations, his confusions, his questions, some of the same problems that had bothered them, or they had asked the same questions about themselves, when later they might find The Shooter at the Glassways and listen to his progress report.

The word began to spread beyond St. Louis and traveled down the River to Big Nig's and to Yeller's and west to Vegas. The Cincinnati Kid's itch to sit down with Lancey Hodges became the talk.

Unofficially then, The Shooter had become The Kid's mentor and this too was strictly defined by protocol. No one offered suggestions to The Kid directly, this would have been an affront to The Shooter; protocol demanded they first speak to The Shooter. The Shooter would then rule on their ideas as being sound or unsound for The Kid.

Unofficial too was the relationship between The Kid and The Shooter. The Kid had not asked for and The Shooter had not offered assistance. But it was regarded as high honor and a very great compliment for anyone in The Kid's class to ask The Shooter for help in sitting down with Lancey Hodges. And The Shooter responded, wearing his new role as an elder of the elite gravely.

The Shooter knew. He remembered Whistling Sam Magee and he knew. It was not a small thing.

The Cincinnati Kid did not know of a single rambling-gambling man who was married. They lived with their women without benefit of wedlock and the women lived like summer birds fluttering around the man but never getting into his core, or even getting close at all. Through the years, though, there had been some that had been together for a very long time.

A woman lived well when her man was off the edge of his stake, putting up with it when the cards were bad and he could not even buy a pot with all the money in the Bank of America. Sex was the most important thing to a rambling-gambling man in his relationship with his woman, and the woman, to run with him, had to be very patient, never demanding, and she had to know how to wait, and when he came to her she had to be ready to give her man sex. She did not have to understand what she was doing for him, and it was not his place to tell her, or woo her, or be anything but gentle with her in his love-making, yet it was not cold or perfunctory and it was rarely premeditated.

Sometimes a woman would try and get between her man and the cards and this was always a dangerous thing for her to do; usually, when this happened, and it did not happen often, but when it did, it put the relationship on ice. So, if the woman could be content to live with him and abide his relatively few demands and it did not bother her to be alone for long periods of time while he was playing cards and she had the patience of an old priest, then it was a working relationship. But if the woman tried to deepen it and do anything else with her man, it was no good. She had to understand that the man was a gambler and that his life was all there in the cards and nothing could change that.

The Cincinnati Kid's woman was a small delicately built honey blonde from the Arkansas hills where there are a lot of honey blondes. She had dark eyes and a small mouth and a quiet way. She had drifted into St. Louis several years before and worked as a waitress before meeting The Kid. She was young and placid and not eager and she rarely talked, being content to go to the movies or read *Life* and *Look* and *Time* and *The Post,* and when she wasn't reading or going to the movies or fixing something to eat on the burner, she would sit at the window dressed in her slip, her hair long and clean and sing mountain songs to herself and rock back and forth and stare down into Broom Street.

Sometimes the men would rate their women and The Kid's woman always came out near the top. And they did not miss The Kid's quiet way with his woman either. He was free with his change (which is what they called all money given to the woman, or that was used for anything except gambling, when it was the stake) and this was a sure sign of a good relationship.

And sometimes it would happen, but rarely, that the women would get together when a game was in one of their rooms or in an apartment and they would go to one side and talk while the game was played out. The women generally got along with each other, but there were times when a woman would find it hard to be nice when she knew her man was losing. Sometimes it would happen that the woman would get mean and jealous and yell at her man, but this did not happen often and this was one of the good things they had to say about The Kid's woman. She never talked loud.

Usually the woman was picked up when the man was way off the edge of his stake and with a big roll. At that time he would attract the best his roll could afford and then, if he went down, and the relationship was a good one, she would go down with him and he would have a good thing going for him while he was in hock and could not even buy a pot with all the money in the Bank of America.

The Shooter was living with a blonde who was not more than thirty and who was considered beautiful; she got a big play when the talk at the Glassways turned to women, partly because they believed she had gone to college. They never asked her, this was speculation on their part from the fact that she read thick books and she dressed New York. The Shooter had been with his woman a long time now and it was a good relationship, and the woman was admired for sticking with the big man while he was on the edge. He had been down a long time but this did not seem to bother her at all.

But the usual, the common denominator — give or take a few years in their ages and advantages or disadvantages in the individual, this one would be pretty with no chest, or that one would be stacked very nicely but stupid, or loud, or jealous, or all three — the common denominator would be Christian, The Kid's woman, twenty-two, rather plain, but refreshing enough to get by, distant and not at all aware of her man except that what she was doing was important to him, and that he felt, in what way she was not sure, she was important to him.

The Kid lay sprawled in bed covered by a sheet, the shades drawn tight against the hot glare of the St. Louis afternoon sun, and could not get to sleep, though he had slept very little during the last two days. The poker hands he had played at Hoban's kept coming back and he could not lose them. From the deep, deep dark of the room, he listened to the sounds of the world moving around him, beyond him. A breath of air caught the bottom of the shade, brushed it, and a streak of golden sunlight flashed instantly into the room. Then, as quickly, the air sucked the shade back into position and it was dark again. He listened too for the soft pad of the woman moving around the rooms and he could see her in his mind, in her slip, hair streaming down her back. She settled into a chair and began to thumb through the pages of a magazine, and he could tell from the rhythmic regularity of the turning pages that she was only looking at the pictures and the ads and not reading. He turned over. The crackle of the pages stopped and the room was cool with silence.

After a while, The Kid spoke. "It's all right. You don't have to act like a cat. You don't disturb me."

"I'm sorry, honey."

"That's all right."

The pages began again. He opened and closed his eyes, and the poker hands came back and he knew then that he was not going to sleep. He got up, slowly, and saw that she was holding the magazine carefully, so it would not make a sound and looking at him with a questioning look on her face, and he shook his head in reply to that look on her face and to reassure her that she was not the cause of his not sleeping. "I'm overtired," he said.

She waited, looking at him as he sat on the side of the bed, feet on the floor, head down, hung over. "Why don't you have a nice hot bath? I could give you a rub down and then you could have a nice hot bath, an' then maybe you could sleep."

He didn't answer, but remained hung over the side of the bed. Very slowly, he nodded his head. "All right," he said. "I'll try it. I would take a pill, but they drug me so, and I gotta get into shape."

She moved, tossing the magazine to one side and walked into the bathroom. In a moment he heard the water running hard into the tub. She opened the medicine cabinet and he knew she was taking out the alcohol. She came back into the bedroom and stood before him, holding the bottle, and waited. When he didn't move, she put the bottle on the table, and he turned, putting his face in the pillow. She went right to work on his shoulder muscles and her strong country girl's hands got right to where it was the worst.

"I saw The Shooter's woman," she said. "We went to a picture show last night. We saw a very good picture."

"What was the name of it?" he asked.

"It was French. I can't say it. But it was a good picture."

"A French picture in St. Louis?" he asked.

"Uh-huh. That little theater over near to Market Strit. They serve coffee in the basement and everybody sits around like they was in a front room, drinkin' coffee and talking. It was nice."

"I didn't know you ran with The Shooter's woman," he said.

"I see her once in a while."

"How often?"

"Ony about, well, when you and The Shooter are in the same game."

"You like her?"

"Uh-huh."

"Whose idea was it to go see the French picture?" The Kid asked.

"Hers. I'd never have the nerve to go in a place like that," she said, working still on his neck and shoulders.

"Why not?"

"I'd be ashamed to. Not knowing French, Kid."

"You think everybody in St. Louis knows French? That ain't even so in New Orleans," The Kid said.

She didn't reply.

"Didn't they have subtitles?" he asked.

"Uh-huh, but I didn't know that before I went," she said, and stopped to pour more alcohol into her palm.

"Did you like the picture?"

"I didn't at first, to tell you the truth."

"Why not?"

"You know, I felt bad and all. All around us there were people talking in French, at least it sounded like French, and I was a little starchy about it."

"Because you didn't know French."

"Uh-huh."

"But then you got over it."

"Uh-huh."

"And you liked the picture."

"Well, not exactly. Not at first, Kid," she said.

"Why not?"

"Well, I ain't one to be prissy and stiff about how people live, but it bothered me that the women in the picture behaved the way they did, walking around with no clothes on, well, not *no* clothes, but you could see their bosoms clear as light."

"Did it bother you?"

"It did. It surely did."

"Then you started to enjoy the picture?"

"Uh-huh."

"When?"

"When I realized that it was probably a true picture of the way things are, in France, I mean." She started working on his back, digging in hard into the long flat muscles and down to the small. "Then I didn't pay any attention to it. I just started to keep up with the words as they flashed on the screen at the bottom of the picture. And kept up with the story."

"What was the story about?"

"Well," she said, turning for more alcohol, "it wasn't a straight clean story the way other pictures are. There were lots of things I didn't understand."

"American pictures," The Kid said. "You mean American pictures."

"Yes," she said. "I guess I do."

"Did The Shooter's woman like it?"

"She seemed to. Did you know she speaks French?"

"I dint know," The Kid said. "But I ain't surprised."

"This girl in the picture was a tart, and she got into trouble and went to this famous lawyer and — " Christian paused.

"And what?"

"She was a disgusting little thing. But she was kinda pretty. She pulled up her dress and showed her parts to the lawyer and said something like, 'You can have all you want if you'll take my case.' You see, Kid, he didn't want to defend her at first."

"But when he saw what she was offering, he took it," The Kid said. "I bet he regretted it. Like trying to catch a fifth card for your straight hand. You go for it and pay the price and then it ain't as advertised. It takes a lot of guts to back away from a promise of something good when you know it ain't going to work out."

She slapped him playfully on the rump and turned away. "I'll just turn off the bath water," she said.

He did not move. He had his face buried in the

pillow and the good clean smell of the alcohol on his body and neck was cool to his nostrils. He closed his eyes and the poker hands stopped running through his head. He did not hear her come back into the bedroom.

He woke up the next morning at eleven and though he had slept hard, he was clear-headed; after speaking her name, and listening for a moment, he realized he was alone and that she had probably gone out for something. He was refreshed and he was glad that he had not taken a pill. He made his own coffee and took a cup with him into the bathroom while he shaved, then came back into the kitchen where he fixed eggs and bacon. He listened to the news and he did not have any trouble putting cards out of his mind.

At noon, when Christian had not yet returned, and feeling irritable and nervous, he left the rooms and went for a walk. He found St. Louis, once he looked at it, a spacious city, a steady succession of framed tableaus opening before him with each corner; a gothic spire atop a white limestone church, solemn, inviting visitations by the Holy Ghost; a soft movement of oaks, green, rich with springtime luxury, throwing dapple shade on a red-bricked street; New Orleans wrought iron arching over worn brownstone steps and ending before a massive door, and above this, the lintel, both door and lintel made of hand-hewn valley oak; a second story in a Victorian house of gables with leaded windows; a splendid façade of a half dozen delta columns, the shafts small and white and worn smooth as old metal and the capital wreathed in a garland of hand-carved oak leaves. All of it, not unlike his home town of Cincinnati, eased his irritation and nervousness some. A hot city, slaked out on the banks of the Mississippi, with too much of its muscle showing to be a dignified city.

He stopped in a beer joint and ordered a bottle of Bud. He sipped it slowly, because he did not want it to give him a quick lift and then drop him. He might be tempted to have another, and he felt that he was in training and could not afford to have two. A Negro boy was shining a man's shoes in the corner of the room and slapping his rag, making a rhythmic hungry little sound that was light and easy and counter to the rhythms the boy heard in his own head. When the Negro boy was finished he asked The Kid if he wanted a shine.

"No."

"A singy-song, then, suh, 'cause I play good."

"Play what?" The Kid asked.

"Listen to this."

The shoeshine boy whipped out a Prince Albert tobacco can with the lid torn off and flattened down at the top. He gave the can a tentative shake and a soft sound like the rustle of dry leaves came forth. He then took out a second can exactly like the first.

This second can, when shaken, gave a sharper rattle like a collection of dry bones in a field sack.

The boy held up the first can. "Dry corn in this 'un." He then held up the second can. "Blue shale stone from th' river in this 'un."

The shoeshine boy stood perfectly still a moment and then slowly, rolling his eyeballs up into his head and closing his dusty, thick lids, began to shake the can filled with dried corn, twisting his wrists, flinging his hands out in a snapping motion, and at the same time began to sing. His left hand, holding the shale stone can, chorded, and emphasized and accented the soft whisper in the corn can. The bartender walked over to listen. Leaning on fat arms he watched the boy.

The boy sang in a warm liquid voice, shuffling his feet slightly, rattling the corn can, expressively and lightly annotating his rhythms with the stone can; a small, delicate, pure voice. It was a sad song and the rhythms of the corn and stone cans never varied, except for the brief break when the boy bent over his hands and, shaking his wrists, concentrated on his rhythmical balance. Then the last verse, a chorus, and finish. It was catfish music created on the spot.

"Thank you," The Kid said.

"Y'wel'cum, suh." The shoeshine boy ducked his head.

"That was nice," The Kid said. "Where did you learn to do that?"

"I pick it up from Hurmin."

"Who is Herman?"

"Mah frien' lives to the river."

"Is he a good friend?"

"Ah don' know 'bout that, suh. He jest a frien who teach me some things." The boy did not look at the bartender or The Kid.

"I don't want a shine, but here's a quarter," The Kid said.

"Thank you, suh!"

"And here's another dime, Bozo." The bartender turned and rang up a NO SALE on the cash register and flipped the dime to the shoeshine boy.

"Nice little nigger kid, ain't he?" the bartender said contentedly, as the shoeshine boy ran out of the door into the hot streets.

The afternoon wore on into the dead, humid heat of a St. Louis afternoon that is worse than the afternoons in New York City, but not as bad as the afternoons in Chicago; he walked on and on and on, getting himself tired from the extra activity that he was not used to and finally ended up back on Harold Street. He was very tired by then and he hurried to the Valley Steam Baths and was quick getting out of his clothes and into the steam room.

He tried to read a paper but he could not concentrate. Musial was not hitting and this disturbed him; the Cardinals were not going anyplace unless Musial began to hit — and hit big. He put the paper aside and wondered if St. Louis was going to wind up like

Pittsburgh and not get a decent club and stay in the second division for thirty years.

The Shooter and Pig were great baseball fans and never missed a game unless they were playing cards. The Kid liked it, but he had been brought up on the Reds. It was always hard for him to pull for the Cards when they came to town. A half hour of hot steam and he found an empty table and stretched out, closing his eyes.

"Cincinnati Kid." The voice was Jansen's, and then he felt the big, sure, flat, spatulate fingers working on him. "Hello, Kid, they running for you?"

"All aces."

"Good-good." And then the miracle-working fingers of the man began to dig into the shoulder muscles that are always the first to get it in a big game and probed into the neck. He fell asleep.

The Kid went directly to the cold stalls and, always a little fearful that the shock would give him a heart attack, stepped in and pulled the chain that sent down a torrent of ice-cold water over his body and in a few seconds he was over it and it was good. He raised his face to the strong stream, but unable to take much of it on his eyes, he finished.

He went back to the rooms, picked up his woman and they caught a cab to the new restaurant over on Market Street and ate a quiet dinner of steak and cheese and a cold lettuce heart. He drank one bottle of Bud and did not have his usual Scotch sour.

"How'd you sleep, Kid?" She asked.

"I slept okay."

"I hope you don't mind my not being there when you woke up."

"No, I don't mind," he said. The Cincinnati Kid looked at the woman across the table. "I'm going up against a big game soon."

She raised her eyes and looked at him a long time and nodded. "I heard about it," she said.

Ordinarily that would have ended it, but he could tell there was something on her mind. And it had to do with her not being in the rooms when he woke up.

"What's the matter?" The Kid asked.

"It's a very big game, I hear," she said.

"Yes."

"Will it be long?"

"Why?"

"I thought — "

"Thought what?"

"I'd go home and see Mama."

The Kid liked her, but he thought about his stake. A thousand wasn't very much to sit down with with Lancey. But he didn't want to explain this to her. Their relationship had never developed to the point where he could talk to her and confide in her. Even if this had been something he wanted in their relationship, it had not gotten that far.

"I wouldn't be able to give you much change," The Kid said, not wanting to say it. He had always

46 ♠

given her whatever she needed so long as it didn't drop his stake too low.

She looked up quickly. "Oh, I wouldn't want much. I could take a bus. That would be all right."

"Well," The Kid said, reluctant to give in, yet not wanting to cheese it by explaining about Lancey, "you can't go home without bringing your Mama something nice."

"That won't be necessary, Kid," she said softly. "Mama wouldn't mind."

They ate in silence a moment and he finished his Bud and put the glass down carefully, making a wet ring on the white tablecloth. "Look," The Kid said, "would a hundred fish do you? I mean, would it be enough for the bus and something for your Mama?"

"That would be fine, Kid." She spoke without looking at him. "Jest fine."

"All right," The Kid said. "When would you want to go?"

"No reason for not going right now," Christian said. "Unless — " she lowered her eyes.

"Unless what?"

It was one of the things he liked about her, her shyness and her quiet modesty. "Unless you want to go back to the place and go to baid."

"Well — " The Kid said, feeling something stir inside of him. "Do you want to? Would you like it?"

She blushed. "Uh-huh. I'd like it."

"Okay," he said tightly. "Okay."

They quickly finished their dinner and rode a cab back to the rooms. Though they had been living together for nine months, they were both a little nervous and a little embarrassed. Nothing between them had ever been spoken. It had never gone to more than a touch on his part, or a familiar kiss and she was willing.

It was good for both of them and later with the night no further away than the other side of the window shade, they were alone and they smoked. They were very quiet and neither of them spoke for a long while and both of them knew that something had to happen or this was the end.

She was the first to move. She stood up in the darkness of the room and he could see her plainly as she moved about the room. Her breasts were high and full. She had a little belly and the navel was like a bad patch on a tire, slightly protruding with mysterious intertwinings; she shivered as a breath of air caught her dampened body.

"What will you do?" he asked finally.

"Something or other."

"I mean, will you stay with your Mama now?"

She did not answer for a long time, moving to the window and raising the shade and standing well back in the dark room, so that the street lights would not shine on her, and then sat down in her chair, tucking her leg under her as she always did. "I might as well stay home with Mama."

"Why, might-as-well?" he asked from the bed.

"I never did like city streets."

"Oh."

"Uh-huh. The promise didn't fulfill itself for me."

"Promise?"

"Come to the city and all."

"Oh," he said. "I see."

"Ah don't know if you do or not, Kid," she said. "I'm country, an' I used to sit there in the hills and study the wishing book. It was all a promise."

"Oh," he said. "I see."

"No, you can't. You're city, Kid, and I'm country. You probly grown up with electric lights and a flush toilet. You can't see."

The Kid didn't answer, but stared at the flash of lights against the walls where the passing cars on Broom Street threw their beams through the open window.

"What will you do?" Christian asked.

"Well, I've got that big game."

"Ah heard he's The Man for you."

"Yes."

"Ah heard it all from The Shooter's woman today. You been coming on strong a long way. This is your time," she said.

"Yes," he said guiltily, from the deep darkness, overwhelmed that he had his time and guilty in the presence of someone he cared for who understood that he had it and all this while she had missed the promise.

"I might win," The Kid said. "There would be a lot of money."

"You'll win," she said, and for the first time since he had known her, her voice was flat, hard and suggested the iron that would be underneath the modesty and quiet way.

And then because she had to try, because she had to know that she tried, and though the words were like hot pebbles coming out of her throat, she turned to him.

"Come home with me to Mama's, Kid."

The Kid didn't answer, not right away, and lay perfectly still. "I'm sorry," he said finally.

"Uh-huh, I know you are, honey," Christian said with gentleness in her tone. "I know it."

Neither of them spoke as she moved around the room and packed her clothes. When she finished and had dressed herself and combed her hair, she sat down in her chair, pulling it closer to the window, and looked down into the street. When she was quiet, The Kid got up and dressed and when he was finished, he walked to the dresser where he kept his stake in the bottom drawer and took out the money. He took five clean twenty-dollar bills and snapped the crisp leaves gambler style without thinking about what he was doing and put the money on top of the dresser. Then he took two more and put them with the others.

"I wish there could be more," he said.

"That's all right," she said, getting up and taking

the money. She tucked it small and put it inside her change purse.

They stood together in the room and she looked around. "I guess that's everything."

He picked up her suitcase and he stood a moment holding the door and she stood still in the middle of the room looking around. "I don't guess I'll ever forget these rooms, Kid."

"I don't guess I will either," he said.

"You going to move?"

"Either way, I guess I'll move. If I win, it won't be good enough. If I lose, I lose it all."

"That's what The Shooter's woman said."

He got it then and it was hard for him to take.

"Are you doing this, so you won't be a burden on me? I mean, to get off my back, in case I lose?" he asked. "Is that it?"

She was very slow in answering. "I don't want to say anything I don't mean, Kid," she said.

"Then don't."

"But since you asked, that's the way things are." She nodded. "I was planning to go back to Mama's anyway and think things out."

"And this helped you to decide?"

"Uh-huh."

"Then don't go," The Kid said, putting the suitcase down.

"No, this is your time," she said firmly. "Now, you go on, honey, and you play The Man. I'll be at Mama's."

They took a cab down to the bus station and he bought her all of the picture magazines and sat in the waiting room with the suitcase between his legs and neither of them spoke until her bus was announced and he went with her to the platform, seeing that it was one of the old buses, which the company used to run over the old country roads and put her suitcase in the luggage rack overhead and made sure she was comfortable.

"Good-by, Kid," she said.

"Good-by, Christian," he said. "Say hello to your Mama for me."

He stepped through the door and did not look back until the last moment and then he waved to her, and she waved to him through the window.

There was an awful moment right after she had disappeared when the bus pulled out, when he felt lonelier than at any other time in his life. But he knew, even as he thought about it, that it was passing and would not linger around and bother him, and when it passed over him like a suffocating cloud, and he was free of it, he knew she had done the right thing. There were no holds on him now. He understood then, as he walked back to the rooms, why he had been nervous and irritable that day and why he had taken the long walk. He had been worrying about her. He stopped dead still in the middle of the sidewalk and examined this thought very slowly and very carefully. It was the first time he had ever worried about anyone except himself.

He did not go to his rooms, but walked on up to the Glassways and had a bottle of Bud with Carey and Wildwood Jones; when The Shooter came in, they shot a little casino and at midnight they had shrimp and salad and he had one more bottle of Bud. They did not talk cards or poker and the casino was not serious; they did not even play for the shrimp and salad, and he went back to his rooms and fell asleep at once.

It began to work on him that he had made a mistake when he awoke the next morning and he was very much aware that he was alone. He managed to put it out of his mind, but he had to work at it, and by the time it took him to shave and dress, it was gone. He sat down to his coffee and thought about cards and he was on his third cup when the phone rang. It was The Shooter.

"I been spreading the word, Kid. It looks like you're in," The Shooter said. "How do you feel?"

"Fine," The Kid said. "How long before I sit down?"

"A while yet, Kid. A while. Why don't you and Christian come out to the ball game this afternoon? Do you good."

"Christian went home to her Mama," The Kid said, not wanting to say it, but not wanting to lie about it either.

"Oh?" The Shooter said over the line. And then while The Kid waited, The Shooter decided to let it ride. "Well, come on with us anyway. We're over to the Glassways. And you need a relaxing day."

"Who all is going?" The Kid asked. "I wouldn't wanta talk cards today."

"Naw man!" The Shooter said. "Ain't nobody dealing nothing. Pig and Carmody and Carmody's woman is all's going. You better come to the ball game, Kid, cause you ain't going to do yourself any good sitting around doing nothing."

When The Kid didn't reply right away, The Shooter spoke again. "Money is beginning to show for you against The Man, Kid."

"What kind of money?" The Kid asked.

"The word is," The Shooter said quietly, "that you're good enough to take Lancey, if anybody can. Anybody in sight, that is. And Newy and Covey is putting you at even money. I heard Jolly and Spriigi and Big Nig got together over the phone about the game and they thinking about coming."

"Even money, huh?" The Kid questioned. "What about Vegas and Big Nig?" The Kid asked.

"Well," The Shooter said, and The Kid heard the hedge in his voice, "odds is a little longer."

"I'll bet they are," The Kid said. "I'll just bet they're a little longer. Ony about ninety-nine to one, or something like that."

"No, Kid," The Shooter said seriously. "They ain't that long. As a matter of fact, I dint finish telling you. Jolly, Spriigi and Big Nig, when they talk on the phone, put at three to one. I got eight hundred of Big Nig's money at them odds."

"They won't go no shorter than that," The Kid said, respectfully.

"I don't figure," The Shooter said.

"Yeah," The Kid said huskily, looking around the empty rooms and feeling that she was not there all over again. "Yeah."

"You coming to the ball game, Kid?" The Shooter asked.

"All right," The Kid said. "I'll come right down."

"Don't come here," The Shooter said. "We all takin' this cab from here in ten minutes. We'll go ahead to the section and save you a seat."

"Then I'll see you at the section," The Kid said, and he hung up the phone.

He sat down beside the phone and did not move for some minutes as he thought about her. But as hard as he tried he could not kill it off and he got up and left the rooms, trying very hard not to think about Christian.

It was a very good day for a game, and without being aware of it The Kid began to settle down and relax. He caught The Shooter looking at him several times, and once he winked at The Kid.

"I told you, Kid!" The Shooter said. "Ain't this just great!" The big man waved a huge paw out toward the grass of the outfield and up at the sun-filled sky.

They were sitting in a section that was not considered a good place to sit to see the ball game, but
it suited their purpose perfectly; they got the very
hot noon sun and then when it began to get muggy
and stinking hot in the late innings, they were in
the shade. Many people sat in this section and they
were the regulars who had been sitting there for
many years and many knew each other by their first
names, and nearly everybody knew each other by
sight. They were not young or old, and there was
nothing special about them except that they sat in
this section and they were all experts on baseball.
Some of the old fans who had been sitting in the
section for years, who were now retired and did not
have to leave in the fifth or sixth inning to go to
work, brought vacuum bottles of ice water and bas-
kets of food and large sun hats and field glasses and
spent the whole day there; the women talked of
their babies, or their grandbabies, or they knitted, or
they just sat in the sun. If a stranger happened to
push into the section, which did not occur very often,
but did now and then on big games when every seat
in the park was taken, the stranger, if he was baseball wise at all, would soon become aware that he
had gotten into a private family picnic. Nothing was
ever said to the stranger, because if he came back
often enough he would become a regular. It was
very obvious right away if a stranger could become
a regular or not. There was one rule: if he com-
plained about the poor view of the game, he did not

belong there at all. It was not the place for the fan who was able to slip away from his office for one game and wanted a thrill every pitch. Baseball to those in the section was not so much of a thrill of the game as it was a part of life, as unquestioned as working, or sleeping, or eating, and it wasn't a game, it was baseball.

The Kid stripped down to his waist and let the hot early summer sun pour down on his skinny, white body. He was aware that he was in training.

"Who's coming up?" Pig asked.

"Schoendienst," Carmody said.

"A dollar he singles," Pig said.

"I give *you* two to one he singles."

"Make it three to five," Pig said, "and you got y'self a bet."

"Mark it," Carmody said, and the bet was made.

There was a discussion on the mound between the Giants pitcher and the catcher on how to pitch to the batter.

"They walk him, not hit," The Shooter said. "I'm laying it." He took a long pull on his beer.

"I'll take the lay," The Kid said easily. "Three to two he gets a piece of the ball."

"Mark it," The Shooter said, happily, and he yelled for another beer.

The game resumed. The pitcher, a tall, lean, whip-thin youngster who delivered sidearm, checked his sign, stepped on the rubber, set, threw. There was a sharp, satisfying sound of bat and ball meeting, and Mays drifted over with the supreme grace that made his speed look slow and the ball came to him as though drawn there by a magnet.

The bets were paid off. They ordered beer all around while Carmody's woman and The Shooter's woman laid on a very careful film of sun lotion over their faces and arms.

It was a very good game, with the Cards winning and Musial getting a single and a triple and two walks. Mays got a homer that was hit so hard the ball was in the left field stands before Mays reached first base.

The Kid was in good spirits when the game was over and, feeling hot and sticky, went with Pig over to the Y and had a fast game of handball, took a swim and did ten even laps at a steady crawl and then, still with Pig, took a cab over to East St. Louis to Victoria's where, with The Shooter and his woman and Carmody and his woman, they all had steaks.

In the next few days the town began to fill up with important people who had come for the game and also to have some fun and get together and shoot a little casino. Miriam was the first to arrive, then Yeller, and Old Lady Fingers, who hated St. Louis, but who happened to be over the edge of her stake or she wouldn't be caught dead in St. Louis, Jolly and Spriigi was there and someone said that Big Nig was sure to come up the river from Memphis for the game, and when The Kid saw all of them coming into town and when Spriigi told him that Big Nig was a cinch to come, he knew for the first time how really important the game was, both to him and to Lancey.

There was a lot of talk about the game, but when the fraternity saw the size of the gathering delegations, once they got together, they decided to have some fun. Everybody hung out at the Glassways or at Victoria's and during the day they went to the ball games and sat in the section drinking beer and betting on balls and strikes, hits, fouls and flies, and anything else they could think of, until the stadium cops broke it up. But by then the Cards had finished their home stand and went on the road, so nobody cared anyway.

No one asked about Christian, partly because The Shooter passed the word around, and though they all had ideas, none of them was absolutely sure The Kid was carrying a torch for Christian. But it was talked about. Miriam and Old Lady Fingers especially had words about it. But no one was sure. The Kid was relaxed and did not appear to be under any strain at all. Yeller and Spriigi said it was a high compliment to The Shooter who had brought The Kid along so nicely that The Kid was easy and didn't show strain so close to the game.

The Shooter was very careful during those days with all the high-pressure talent showing up in St. Louis, to see that no one talked cards around The

Cincinnati Kid, except when they shot a little casino, and to see that The Kid relaxed when they went to the ball games, and that he worked out every day at the Y, with a swim afterwards. For one of the few times in his life, The Kid ate three meals a day and after nearly a week of this kind of discipline, The Cincinnati Kid began to look good and they all saw it.

Everybody was high on The Kid, but there was very little sentimental money around. And even though Big Nig had pegged the odds himself with his big bet with The Shooter at three-to-one, the odds slipped when money began to show up from Miami Beach, and some very big money from Vegas, where there were people who knew Lancey's play and did not know The Kid's style except by reputation. The odds slipped from three-to-one to seven-to-two. But it wasn't so much of a slip that it scared bettors away and there was still enough Cincinnati Kid money around to grab up the attractive Miami and Vegas seven-to-two and to make The Kid's position respectable.

Five days after Christian left, a Friday, The Kid was sleeping when the phone rang. He had gone to sleep the night before thinking about the weekend and beginning to get a little edgy, not wanting to face the weekend with the Cards on the road and nothing to do but sit around or see a picture. He grabbed the phone, hoping it would be The Shooter and that the game was set.

"Hello?"

"Kid?" It was The Shooter.

"Yeah."

"Listen, Lancey just got word to me through Spriigi that he's ready to sit down with you Monday night."

"Oh." The Kid's voice dropped. He looked out of the window. It looked like rain.

"Something wrong?" The Shooter asked.

"No. I was just hoping that it would be tonight."

"Well," The Shooter said matter-of-factly, "it ain't. It's Monday night, seven-thirty, Dorset Hotel, room three-eleven."

The Kid didn't say anything.

"That don't suit you, Kid, we can always make arrangements for you."

"It's not that," The Kid said, looking out of the window and seeing the first drops of rain on the windowpane. "Dorset's fine. Seven-thirty, room three-eleven. Fine. Fine."

"Kid, you don't sound right." The Shooter said, a hint of concern in his voice.

"No, everything's all right. Like I said, I was just hoping it would be tonight. I hate this waitin' so."

"I know what you mean, Kid," The Shooter said. "But Lancey's only finished that game to the Washburn Hotel yesterday morning. He's gotta have time to get relaxed and all. You wouldn't wanta push him, and him not being right."

62 ♠

"No. I'm not complaining," The Kid said.

"Okay." The Shooter said. "What you wanta do today?"

"I ain't woke up yet, Shooter," The Kid said. "Lemme get an eye opener and I call you back, okay?"

"I'm home," The Shooter said, his voice pleasant again. "You come on over here with me and the woman and we figure out something for the day."

"I call you back," The Kid said.

"See you."

"See you." The Kid dropped the phone in the cradle and rolled back onto the pillow, pulled the sheet up around his neck and stared at the quickening rain, and thought about it.

The Kid had never considered himself or his life beyond his environment. He moved from moment to moment guided by his instinct and he had never made any attempt to understand any world except his own. He was aware though that he had, through his talent with cards, forged a place for himself; but The Kid had never been much of a reader, lacking the curiosity and the patience to find out how a character in a book got on with his life, so his perspective was as narrow and as restricted as the world of cards and stud poker. He had only his own meager experiences to draw on as he tried to project the consequences of the game.

The only thing he had going for him, The Kid

reasoned, was his fair hand at stud poker. And his only thought now was a hope that the game, whatever happened, would not cost him too dear. If he won from Lancey, and if he became The Man, his life would change. Hadn't he told Christian that if he won, it would not be good enough? And if he lost?

That was the part that sobered him as he stepped from the bed and began to move about the rooms making coffee and smoking a cigarette. Would losing take anything away from him? He was, for a moment, almost sorry that he had challenged Lancey.

Why had he done it? He could not, at that moment, answer the question. He had been quite content the way it was before. The challenge and the game, he saw, had already taken Christian away from him and he had not turned a card yet.

He sipped coffee and drew angrily on the cigarette. His jaw tightened. He had been a fool to let Christian go to her Mama's. There had been something underlying and nervous about his whole week and it had not been the game, or Lancey. He read it now for what it was. It was Christian.

He looked at the rain, and sat sipping his coffee and did not move for a long time as he thought about it.

It stopped raining an hour later, but it remained cloudy and threatening. He could not sit still or stay in the rooms and thought he would go down to the Y and work out, but on his way there, he changed his mind and just started walking. At noon he found himself at the zoo and ate hot dogs and drank coffee out of paper cups. At one-thirty he was on the rubbing table at the Valley Steam Baths and Jansen was working on his neck and back.

"Monday night, uh, Kid?" Jansen said.

"Monday night."

"Ya feel good?"

"Great," The Kid said. "Just great."

"I sprung for some of the action."

"Yeah?" The Kid said, a little surprised. "Thank you, Jansen."

"Forget it. Just a yard and a half of that seven-to-two."

"They been holding like that all week, I hear," The Kid said.

"They're very respectable odds, Kid," Jansen said, surprise in his voice. "You don't have to go in ashamed. Them's nice numbers, considering Lancey's The Man and known."

"Been a lot of action?"

"Since the word come around that Lancey had set the time and place. Since then, Kid. I turn my hot rooms into bookie parlors," Jansen said. "This is big time."

"I hope you don't wind up holding," The Kid said.

"Just do right, Kid," Jansen said. "Ain't nobody in the world can snow Cincinnati Kid when he's right. You be right, Kid, don't worry," Jansen said confidently.

"I hope so," The Kid said.

"Kid," Jansen said seriously, "I know you a long time. Long time. How long we been playin' fifteen-cent stuff down to Hoban's, and all?"

The Kid didn't answer.

"Long enough I know you like I know your trapezoids," Jansen said in the tone of a man who is sure. "You be right. Roll over, an' I get them rectus abdominis. That's where skinny guys like you get it, in the gut. You be right, Kid, don't worry."

The Kid rolled over, feeling warm inside all of a sudden. "Yeah," he said. "I'll take him."

"Sure," Jansen said. "See what I mean?"

At a quarter of three, feeling his nervousness and his indecision falling away from him like dirty shower water, The Kid left the Valley Steam Baths and walked to the bus station. He had two chicken salad sandwiches and a cup of coffee while he waited for the bus. At the last moment he remembered The Shooter and slipped into a phone booth. There was no answer at the big man's room in the Mills Hotel, and The Kid left a message with the clerk.

"Just tell him The Cincinnati Kid said he would be there on Monday night."

"You be there on Monday night, Mister Kid, suh."

"Yes. That's the message," The Kid said. "For The Shooter."

"I tell him, suh, you The Cincinnati Kid and you be there on Monday night."

"That's right."

"All right, suh."

"Thank you," The Kid said and hung up.

He had to run for the bus and just made it. Jansen's massage had relaxed him more than he knew and he fell asleep almost at once and did not wake up until the bus was all the way across southwestern Missouri and nearing the Arkansas line in the Ozark country.

It was ridge and valley country, with huge stands of pine known locally as possum wood and used extensively for building barns, sheds and only rarely for homes, since the wood does not weather well; most of the houses were made of oak taken from the lower vales where they had been growing for hundreds of years. In the White River regions, through which The Kid passed, there were deep, tortured cuts in the limestone and occasionally he could see caverns and caves Indians had used for quartering in winter, and he remembered Christian had told him the caves were considered haunted by her and her friends when they were children. The Kid had been there before, but the country was slower than he remembered it. Once in a while the bus would pass an old truck or car on the road, but except for these isolated contacts with movement and civilization, the bus was alone on the newly paved road. It was not true farm country, but he did pass cleared ground on occasion. He could not tell what was being grown and he was not curious. He was not uncomfortable in the countryside, but he was alien to it, and did not understand it. However, he saw that it was beautiful and soft and, as he had done the time before, he yielded to it, letting it absorb him, giving no resistance.

About eight in the morning there were increasing signs of life as the bus moved deeper and deeper into the Ozarks. At nine, exactly, for the bus was on time, The Kid got off at Tate, which is a small crossroads community supporting Eureka Springs. Ignoring the stares of the curious bench sitters lounging before the General Store and Post Office, he entered the sweet-sour-smelling, dark place and bought several packages of cigarettes.

"You been here before," the storekeeper said in a direct, sharp-eyed way, that was both challenging and questioning.

"Yes," The Kid said.

"I knowd."

The Kid said nothing.

"It was you and Christian Craigie."

The Kid paid for his purchase and nodded, returning the stare.

"She just come home from St. Lou a few days ago."

"I know."

"You come to fetch her?"

"Do they still live up on the hill?"

"Boy, Craigies have been on that hill for over a hundred years." The storekeeper turned away to the cash drawer and glanced up at The Kid from time to time as he made change. He put the silver on the counter and looked directly at The Kid. "Take the road here to the side of the store. Two miles on up. That's the place."

As The Kid stepped out of the door and off the stoop, he heard the storekeeper speak to the bench sitters. "He's Christian Craigie's."

It was a steep climb in places, and level in places, and he remembered certain things about the road as he passed them, coming onto a possum wood pine that had a huge rust ring around the base and he recalled asking Christian about it. Further on, he passed a limestone cave where Christian had played as a child, and then rounding a slight bend, he saw the vale below, clearly and distantly, and not mist-covered as it had been the first time he saw it.

It took him the better part of an hour to make the climb and the walk and then he was at their gate. The dog came out to greet him, fulfilling its duty as watchman and then retreated as The Kid loosened the latch and stepped inside.

The Craigie house was placed on the top and a little to one side of a hillock that gave a perfect view of the surrounding countryside. He had no doubt that he had been observed coming up the road. Then he saw Christian rounding a path that ran off to one side of the house. She carried two five-gallon milk cans slung in a yoke over her shoulder and he recalled that it was a daily chore to bring water up from the spring at the bottom of the hillock to prime the hand pump in the kitchen. She stopped and stood looking at him and he could not see from the reaction on her face if she was pleased or not.

"Hello, Kid," she said, and started walking toward him with a curiously smooth glide to keep the water in the cans slung on the yoke from slopping out.

"Hello, Christian. Can I help you?"

"No, it's just a little way on, and taking it off my shoulders would be worse than taking it on in."

She gave him a quick, brief smile and turned away and he followed her up the path.

"Papa," Christian said, stopping at the bottom step and turning to look at him, "don't know about us. I mean —"

"I understand," The Kid said.

They walked around the side porch to the kitchen door which was opened by Mrs. Craigie. She showed no surprise at seeing The Kid, but she did look at him sharply, and much like the direct, quick stare The Kid had seen in the storekeeper.

"Eric has come to see me, Mama." Christian said.

"Put the water over there, Christian," Mrs. Craigie said. "How do, Eric."

"Hello, Mrs. Craigie," The Kid said.

The two women worked at the water cans, with

Mrs. Craigie lifting them off the yoke and onto the drain sink near the hand pump. The Kid then became aware of the steaming pots on the wood stove. To one side, on the table were a half dozen hampers of small stem green beans. As soon as they had finished with the water cans and Christian had put away the yoke, both women turned to the table and began to snip stems and cut the beans, putting them into the steaming pots.

"Here we were right in the middle of canning," Christian explained, "and we lost suction on the pump."

"Oh," The Kid said.

"There's coffee," Mrs. Craigie stated, not pausing in her work. "And sour ham and bread in the warmer, if you're hungry, Eric. We can't stop now. These are spring beans and you have to cook 'em and can 'em fast."

"Mama likes to can early beans rather than the big, summer, late beans," Christian added.

"They're tenderer," Mrs. Craigie said.

"Go on, Kid," Christian said, "if I know you, you didn't eat anything."

"All right," The Kid said. He put his jacket to one side and turned to the stove, feeling relaxed and comfortable in the big spacious kitchen; comfortable too in that he knew where the cups and the spoons were, and the milk in the chill box in the floor. He poured himself a cup of coffee and made a sandwich of thick cornbread and tart ham that was sweet-sour and quite different from sweet smoked ham and sat down to watch them work.

"How's The Shooter?" Christian asked.

"Fine." The Kid said.

"You haven't played yet, have you?" Christian asked, looking directly at him.

"Monday," The Kid replied. "We play Monday night."

"It must be exciting," Christian said.

"I'm nervous, if that answers your question."

She laughed, and looked at her mother. "I can't imagine The Cincinnati Kid being nervous about anything."

Mrs. Craigie, her hands flying, glanced down only when she reached for another handful of beans, made a polite approving sound in her throat.

Christian dropped her eyes to her work and looked up at The Kid shyly. "I told Mama and Papa about The Man. And all."

"Oh," The Kid said and swilled down the last of his coffee. "Where is Mr. Craigie?"

"To the barn," Mrs. Craigie said. "We're going to be at this for another hour or two, Eric, and I can't let Christian go. Why don't you go down and say hello to Christian's Papa." Mrs. Craigie looked at her daughter. "She didn't tell me we were having company, 'r I would never have started canning."

"I'm sorry," The Kid said. "I should have let you know I was coming. But to tell you the truth, I decided in a hurry."

"We welcome you, Eric." Mrs. Craigie said formally.

"Thank you. I guess I will go down and talk with Mr. Craigie." He stood and, leaving his jacket on the back of a chair, slipped out of the kitchen door and down the back path toward the barn. He saw Mr. Craigie in the cowlot at the side of the barn the moment he was free of the house.

Mr. Craigie greeted him with a gruff, too brief "Hello," The Kid thought and continued to pitch manure onto the pile in the corner, banked against the barn side. He worked a long-handled shovel easily, using every bit of leverage he could with his right hand on the knob of the handle. It was rhythmic and there was no wasted motion, or heavy swinging of the torso or shoulders. Mr. Craigie did not stop until he had finished scraping the concrete floor of the barn and it was clean and the last half shovelful of manure was on the pile. He then took a bucket and dipped water from the trough and washed the floor down. In all this time, perhaps fifteen minutes, Craigie had not once turned and looked at The Kid.

"You seen Christian?" Craigie asked, looking directly at The Kid, stopping still in the middle of the cowlot.

"Yes. She's helping her mother can," The Kid said.

Craigie stood still a moment, looking off over the vale where several brown and white spotted cows

moved contentedly in the morning sun and then
cocked his head to one side, turned and spoke to
The Kid.

"You going to marry Christian?"

The Kid stared back with his poker face, with his
stud face, blank, expressionless, reaction to this
checking of a cinch, this challenge that was now up
to him to raise the cinch or fold his cards; he did
not hurry with his answer as he coolly and calmly
ran over the question and examined the percentages.

Craigie remained perfectly still. The Kid decided
to raise, and tapped the cinch-checking question
softly.

"Do you have any objections if I do, or if I
don't?" The Kid asked.

Craigie walked over to The Kid, his knee-high
boots sucking in the muddy, urine-drenched cowlot.
"Son," he said easily, "that sounds like a smart
alecky answer."

"You want to look at it from my side first, or are
you going to just go ahead with your mind made
up?" The Kid replied.

"I'm considered a fair man, son."

"Christian has said you were."

"I don't know much about you."

"No. Not unless Christian has told you some
things."

"Some," Craigie said. "She told us some."

"You want the histry, I guess," The Kid said,
feeling the pressure building, as it always did when

he had raised a checking cinch and was not sure if he had been right or not. "I met Christian about a year and a half ago. Less, maybe. I was playing in this stud game in a hotel in Hot Springs and she was a waitress in the coffee shop."

"Fifteen months ago was when she was to Hot Springs working to the hotel," Craigie said.

"We went out," The Kid said. "Right after that we come here for the first time. The last time."

"I remember," Craigie said.

"I went on back to St. Louis and then a little while later, I saw her again. We got together."

Craigie nodded, his breath whistling through his thin, long nose. "Living together?"

"Yes," The Kid said slowly, turning over his hole card, letting the light of day come upon that secret that, until then, only he had known.

"She says you're good to her."

The Kid looked at Craigie, remembering that Christian had said he did not know, but of course he had known. A father, a parent, cannot be deceived so easily. He would know.

"How come she come back this time?" Craigie asked. "Is she going to have a baby?"

"Not that I know of."

"You two have a fight?"

"No."

"— Is there a reason at all?" Craigie asked, his question coming fast.

"Look, Mr. Craigie," The Kid said, "let me and Christian find out a few things, then maybe I won't have to answer your questions. Maybe they'll be answered."

Craigie did not answer for a while and looked down at his muddy boots. "It's true, she's growd. I saw that when she lit out for Hot Springs. And I don't know much about gambling fellers."

"I don't think what I am — do for a living — has anything to do with me and Christian," he said.

"I don't understand gamblers."

"Then we're even, because I don't understand farmers," The Kid said.

"You say things that are smart alecky, but they're not. I don't feel they are smart alecky," Craigie said, his breath whistling through his nostrils.

"Well, I can't take into account what somebody's going to feel every time I say something. I just bet 'em as they come off the top."

"Are you a believer, son?"

"In what?"

"Religion."

"No."

"Christian was raised in a Christian home."

"Is that so. I didn't know. I'm not aware of the difference."

"And you only play cards for a living?" Craigie asked.

"Only cards."

"I never played a card game in my life. Never had them in the house that I know of," Craigie said. He looked sharply at The Kid. "Who is this feller Christian says you're going to play that's so important?"

"He's the king of the stud poker players."

"And you going to play him?"

"Yes."

"Are you any good, son?"

"I'm this good. The king, this man, has got to play me," The Kid said.

"You put it to him, did you?"

"Yes."

"What happens if he don't play you?"

"Then everybody will know he ran out and I will be the king," The Kid said.

"That important to you?"

"I been trying to figure that out ever since I set it up," The Kid said.

"How long you been card playing?"

"All my life."

"Because of money?" Craigie asked.

"Not really," The Kid said, lighting a cigarette and offering Craigie one, and putting the pack away when it was refused. "I can make a lot of money just by playing fools who think they're good enough to win from me."

"Take advantage of them, is that what you mean?"

"Yes, that's what I mean."

"Christian said you never was much worried about money." Craigie said, "I been worried about money most of my life. Up until I figured out that it wasn't so important."

"No, it's necessary, but it isn't too important," The Kid said. "I learned that a long time ago."

"You did, huh? And I just learned it," Craigie said. "Well, how come you wanta play this king feller?"

The Kid thought a long time, taking deep, even puffs on the cigarette, glancing now and then out over the vale and down at the cows. "Ambition, I guess," he said finally. "Like that — ambition, maybe."

"Is it aspiration to be the king 'r just uncertainty about the future?"

"I ain't looking for security, if that's what you mean," The Kid said.

"Not trying to lock something up, tight, and nail it down?" Craigie asked.

"Everybody wants to do that," The Kid said. "That would figure into it. But that isn't all of it."

"Are you doing it for fun, then? Just to see if you can be king?"

"No, it's important to me."

"Now, son," Craigie said easily, "which is more important to you, this king business, or Christian?"

The Kid flipped the cigarette into the cowlot and straightened up. "If you got the guts to ask that question, Mr. Craigie, I've got the guts to answer it. Christian, if you came right down to it, is not as important as doing what I have to do."

"No," Craigie mused to himself, but loud enough for The Kid to hear, "you ain't no innocent."

"I'm surprised to hear that you thought I might be."

"Well, son, I had to know."

"What?"

"How you felt about my Christian. I got to get on down to the vale now. I wouldn't mess around the kitchen until they're finished. Mrs. Craigie never did like people around when she was canning."

"Just a minute," The Kid said sharply. "What is it you think you know?"

"Son, there never was a man worth a damn to my mind that let a woman — his woman — stand in the way of a thing he had to do."

The Kid stared at the weathered, lined face.

Craigie took a few steps away and turned and looked at The Kid. "I'd appreciate it if you'd try and explain how you make your living. I'd like to know about that. I'd like to know what Christian will be living like."

"I'll try," The Kid said. "But don't expect too much. I understand it and I think it's because it comes natural to me. But I don't know if you can make anything out of it, because there isn't anything to come out of it except my own feelings."

"You take Christian, when her Mama lets go of

her, and tell her I said you should go to the old
limestone bridge and swim. It'll be hot today. It's a
good place I'm telling you about."

"I'll tell her."

"Now, I'm going." Craigie said and turned and
waded through the cowlot, climbed the fence near
the barn and disappeared down the path that had
been trod by thousands of cows and hundreds of
people over the years, down into the green valley
floor of the vale.

The Kid climbed the fence and sat on the top rail
and pulled his sunshades out of his pocket and
slipped them on against the glare of the hot, near
noon sun.

He sat a long time and watched Mr. Craigie moving about in the vale below and did not go back up
to the house until Christian called for him to come
and have something to eat.

When he told her about swimming at the limestone bridge, she nodded, and smiled, shyly, as he
remembered she did and hurriedly packed a hamper
of bread, coffee, cheese and sour ham and they walked
through the upper ridges, climbing all the time, until
they were on the top of the highest of the ridges and
near a path that led down into a ravine along a well-
worn path and then to the bridge. Arching from one
side of the ridge, across the ravine to the opposite
side of the ridge, the bridge was silhouetted against
the sky. Beneath it, and covered by the canopy of the
bridge, was the spring. The water bubbled up from

below enough to keep the surface moving gently; the pool spilled off the other side of the bridge and he could not see where it went.

She began to undress. "I had the worst kind of a cold once," she said, "and Mama brought me up here and kept dunking me in and out for three days. Massaging me and dunking me and wrapping me in blankets."

She stepped to the edge of the pool and toed it, as he watched her, then stepped into it up to her knees.

"Did you get rid of the cold?" The Kid asked.

"Nearly drowned and had the skin rubbed off, but I got rid of it. Come on now, Kid. This is just wonderful." She splashed across the pool with quick, strong strokes.

They swam and splashed in the warm water, that was very much hotter at the bottom, and when they came out, there was no appreciative difference in the temperature as they both sprawled on the grass bank in the hot sun.

"Kid, why did you come?" she asked, looking at him, raising up on one elbow.

"Because I had to."

"You must have talked to Papa, and he must have known about us in St. Louis, or he wouldn't have told you about this place."

"He knew — he suspected. I dint want to lie to him."

"Let's not talk any more," Christian said.

"All right."

He was on his back, watching a hawk circle high in the sky and then his vision was blotted out by her face moving over his. He felt water dripping from her hair. He thought for a moment about his talk with Mr. Craigie and he wondered how anything could be more important than this.

They had to leave early because Christian had to help with the final process in the canning, and The Kid worked for two hours putting the finishing twist on the tops of the jars of beans. He washed up afterwards and sat on the porch watching the sunset while Christian and her Mama prepared supper. It was still quite light when Mr. Craigie came up from the barn after milking and they all sat down to the meal.

It was the first time The Kid had been within the warmth of a family circle since he was a child and the sly looks, soft comments and chuckles of Mr. and Mrs. Craigie and Christian among themselves was comforting to The Cincinnati Kid and he responded after the meal, putting on a display of card tricks — flashy deals and stacked decks, taking cards from Mrs. Craigie's pockets — that had them roaring with laughter and amazement for two hours.

Later, while the women were doing the dishes, The Kid sat on the front porch and watched the great Arkansas night envelop the Ozarks in an early summer blanket of quiet.

"Son," Craigie said to The Kid in the darkness,

and soft enough for the rattle of the dishes and the cleaning up to cover his words, "you *are* good. You reckon you're better than this feller, the king?"

"I'm the best," The Cincinnati Kid said softly. "I'm the best man in a stud poker game in the world."

They went to bed early, with The Kid sleeping on a cot in the kitchen which he did not mind and that was an added comfort to him, and he lay there thinking about the kitchens he had slept in when he was a child.

It was sometime during the night that Christian slipped into the kitchen in the dark and got under the covers with him and they both lay there in each other's arms for a long time without talking, content to hold and to feel the presence of the other one.

When she saw the first grayness in the sky and knew that her Papa would be up to milk, she rose and gave him a last kiss.

"I be back after the game, Christian," he said. "You wait here for me and I'll let you know."

"All right, Kid," she said.

There was no reason for him to remain in bed after that and he got up, dressed and slipped out of the house. He was halfway to the General Store in Tate when Mr. Craigie eased into the kitchen and saw the empty cot.

It took The Kid nearly twenty hours to make the return trip on the Sunday bus schedule and he arrived in St. Louis after two A.M. Monday morning. He went straight to the rooms and slept until three-thirty that afternoon.

He took a long time in dressing and messing around, shaving and showering and making several pots of coffee, and feeling himself completely relaxed and fit.

At five the phone rang. It was The Shooter.

"I'd ask you where you been," The Shooter said, "if I wasn't ready to give you ten to one that I knew already. How is she?"

"Fine."

"How *you*?" The Shooter asked, his voice a little more concerned. "Did it do you good or bad?"

"Did me good."

"Ready for the tiger, huh?"

"I'm fit."

"Well, that's the story. Nothing's changed. Everything's been charged and everybody's got their money down. All's needed now is the results."

"Post time is seven-thirty at the Dorset, room three-eleven, right?" The Kid said, smiling.

"Ta, tata-tata-tetata-a!" The Shooter said, sounding like a bugle call for the parade to the post. "He's a machine, Kid, but you can take him if anybody can."

"I can and I will," The Kid said.

"Rough him up in the clinches, Kid. See you."

"See you." The Kid hung up.

He stood up and began to dress. Loafers, silk socks, jockey shorts, loose silk sports shirt, silk trousers, half dozen handkerchiefs, reading glasses, suit jacket and his sunshades. When he was finished, he sat down and had one more cup of coffee and began to grow quiet, putting everything out of his mind. He ran through the multiplication tables through twenty-one times twenty-one and eased off. He divided three numbers into nine numbers; he added and subtracted mixed fractions and then he stood up.

He took his roll from the dresser and reached for the door, he took a last look at the rooms and then he went out.

At seven o'cock, completely at ease now, walking around for a few minutes, he stopped in a drugstore and made two purchases: a large bottle of Murine for his eyes and the largest bottle of Listerine mouth-wash they had. Outside in the street, he looked up and down and saw no one that he knew, and then caught a cab at the corner of Broom.

"Dorset Hotel," The Kid said. "And don't hurry. I want to get to the front door at exactly twenty-five minutes after seven."

"Sure."

It would not do to arrive too early. But he couldn't be late either. At exactly seven-thirty, The Cincinnati Kid walked through the door of room 311.

"Hello, Kid. Glad to know you," Lancey was quick, light on his feet with the same kind of pale, pale eyes The Kid had only instead of blue, Lancey's eyes were gray. He brushed his index finger and his second and third fingers on his right hand together in a nervous habit as if there were sand on them or grit or something that would not brush off. It was the first thing The Kid noticed about him. They shook hands.

"Lancey —" The Kid said. "Pleased to meet you."

"Sure-sure," Lancey said. "Know everybody? Sure-sure."

The Shooter was there looking bigger than usual and somber, almost grave. Pig, Carmody, Carey, Shorty, Corrigan, Wildwood Jones, Old Lady Fingers, Spriigi, Jolly and Miriam all stood around and watched as Lancey and The Kid continued their nervous introductions.

"How you feel?" Lancey asked.

"Great. And you?"

"Fine."

"That's good," The Kid said.

"Yeah," Lancey said. "Feel like playing a little."

"Me too."

"Yeah," Lancey said. "I already looked around, Kid, so if you wanta take a look at things — "

" 'kay," The Kid said. "Fine, Lancey. I'll just do that."

The table was a large walnut gateleg, old and scarred but firm and solid, that had been brought up from the room-service storeroom and there was a blanket underneath a white linen spread that had been tied down under the rim with twine. The surface of the table was flat as a board, tight as a drum and cushioned; the chairs were heavy, straight-backed, from the ballroom, with leather seats and they looked comfortable. There were six large ashtrays. The Kid knew that Old Lady Fingers would not play, and did not think Shorty or Wildwood Jones would either. Shorty had been over the edge of his stake a long time now and had not even bought a fifteen-cent seat at Hoban's and no one really believed that he would ever come back again. Wildwood Jones, along with Corrigan, were draw men and not stud men and they wouldn't be caught dead playing stud unless it was for a twentieth of a cent a point. So it was going to be Lancey, The Shooter, Pig, Carey, Carmody and The Kid.

The Kid finished his inspection of the furnishings and nodded that he agreed to them.

"That table ain't the best, Kid, but — "

The Kid waved his hand at The Shooter's apology. "It's all right, Shooter. Fine. Just fine." Then he looked up quickly at Lancey. "Okay by you, Lancey?"

"Fine, Kid." He brushed his fingers. "Light all right for you?" He nodded to a huge drop cord in the ceiling with a green fan shade around a two-hundred watt Mazda.

"Okay by me," The Kid said. "You?"

"Fine. Excellent."

There was a moment of silence and then Lancey turned to The Shooter, who stood to one side like a big brown bear in his shaggy jacket, all quiet and all serious. "You fixed up things just fine, Shooter," Lancey said. "I appreciate it. All you done and all."

"Yeah, Shooter," The Kid said in quick agreement. "Things is great for a little game."

"That's the way I feel," Lancey said.

"Thank you, gents," Shooter said in a somber, heavy way. "I tried the best I could."

"You did fine, Shooter Man," Lancey said.

"You thought of everything," The Kid said.

"Cards?" The Shooter said, looking from one to the other.

"Fine," Lancey said.

" 'kay," The Kid said.

The Shooter turned and looked at Corrigan. The draw man picked up a small dispatch case and put it on the table, unlocked it and snapped it open. He turned it upside down and spilled thirty decks of cards onto the table. He then stepped back.

"They come from the St. Louis Bridge Club. They been bonded by the club steward and I seen him take them out of the safe. The Shooter, Wildwood, Lady Fingers and me pick 'em up and come right here."

"St. Louis Bridge Club, eh?" Lancey said, with a quick smile at Corrigan and then at The Kid. "That old yard bird Okra still there?"

"That's him," Corrigan said.

"He's an old stud man, Kid," Lancey said.

"I dint know," The Kid said.

"Great man," Lancey said.

Corrigan's face clouded over and he looked at The Kid. "Nobody heard from me what the cards were for, Kid."

Lancey looked at Corrigan and then at The Kid.

"I ain't seen Okra to speak to him for ten years, Kid. That's a fact."

" 'kay," The Kid said. "I know what'cha mean, Lancey."

"Yeah," Lancey said quickly.

After a moment of silence, Lancey and The Kid stepped up to the cards and began looking them over. They examined the seals and the cellophane and sniffed at both ends of the deck for the tell-tale odor of a hot iron and a tampered seal. The Kid found three decks that he did not like and handed them over to Lancey, who agreed without looking at them. And these were tossed back into the dispatch case. Lancey found two decks and The Kid waved them away. They went through the remaining twenty-five decks in the same way. None of the others in the room asked to see the cards or examine them, because it was not really their game. This was for The Kid and Lancey.

When this was done, Lancey looked around, brushing his fingers and then leveled his eyes on The Cincinnati Kid. His voice, when he spoke, was light, almost a whisper and his face was set as if in plaster. "What's your game, Kid?" he asked, following protocol, but knowing that it would be stud.

"Stud?" The Kid said, playing it out.

"Fine by me. Yes, fine." He looked at the others. "Gents?"

Everyone agreed. No one would have suggested anything but what The Kid had asked for. Lancey, being The Man, had first pick of the chairs. Everyone knew he would sit with his back to the windows to avoid the bright light of the rising sun and the daylight. This would mean The Kid would have to sit opposite his man and face the windows. The Kid had known this and there were glances of appreciation for his having thought this out when he put the bottle of Murine on the table before him, along with the large bottle of Listerine.

"I like Pepsodent toothpaste best," Lancey said, politely, conversationally, once they were seated. "The taste lasts longer."

"It bothers the roof of my mouth," The Kid replied politely. And then to soften it a little, The Kid added, "But I guess it's all right."

And then Lancey's reply. "I've used Listerine. It's fine."

None of the others came so prepared. The game would work generally for a few hours, perhaps all night, and then one by one they would retire for the balance of the game and leave Lancey and The Kid to face off. The Shooter would deal, since he could handle cards better than anyone in the Mississippi Valley. They didn't want anything to go wrong with a game like this. They did not want to see cards burned — or have any misdeals. They didn't want anything fancy, they just wanted sureness in the handling of the cards and there was no one better qualified for this job than The Shooter.

"I happen to know The Kid likes brandy and coffee, Lancey," The Shooter said. "Anything special for yourself?"

Lancey rocked back in his chair and balanced himself on two legs. He looked more like a banker than The Kid remembered. He hooked his thumbs into his vest that was buttoned up tight and that showed a neat stripe tie and shirt and that held a gold chain running from one vest pocket through a button hole to another vest pocket. "Why, yes, Shooter," Lancey said. "Crème de menthe frappé. Green."

The Shooter only half turned his head to make sure that Corrigan heard this and then turned back to the table, putting his big flat hands and fingers and two massive thumbs on the table.

"Gentlemen, if there are no objections, I'm the dealer. The room has been contracted for and there will be an ante of ten dollars per chair, per day, until the game is over, with a minimum of twenty dollars per day for the room. Corrigan has supplied the cards at five dollars a deck, with the usual guarantee that should the cards be proven spooked, he pays off the losers."

Everyone including Lancey and The Kid looked up at Corrigan who nodded that it was so.

"Gents?" The Shooter asked, looking from one to the other. "Any questions?"

"Fine by me," Lancey said quickly. "Kid?"

" 'kay," The Kid said.

"Very well," The Shooter said, and continued. "During the breaks for me, Old Lady Fingers has agreed to deal, but she will not be a player because she is over her edge and her charges are the usual three dollars an hour, plus her food, and a five-minute break out of each hour. Gents?"

"Fine, Shooter."

" 'kay," The Kid said.

Once everyone had agreed to Old Lady Fingers,

she stepped forward and tapped The Shooter on the shoulder. "I'll be in my room, Shooter."

She slipped out of the door quietly and no one turned to look at her.

"Gentlemen," The Shooter said soberly, "this is a game of five card stud poker. There is no limit. A dead man has one half hour to raise his roll outside of the game and get back into the play."

This somber note in the introductions over, it was the signal for the players to put their money on the table. At the same time The Shooter turned to take one of the decks of cards.

Every eye in the room went immediately to Lancey's roll. He put five thousand dollars on the table. They turned to see what The Kid would do and he put down his thousand. Despite the disparity of stakes a thousand dollars to a man like The Kid would give him a long ride. But more than anything else, they admired The Kid's confidence in coming into a big game like this one with only a thousand. It was a good sign to all of them that The Kid's mood was right, *just* right, to play The Man.

They stacked their money neatly, in ones, fives, tens and twenties, folded once over so they would not have to look down and worry about taking more than one bill at a time. Pig unloosened his belt. Carmody sighed and held a deep breath. Carey sat perfectly still and waited, eyes down. The Kid kept his hands on the table. He wanted them to see that he was not nervous. And they all saw this and so did Lancey.

The Shooter ripped the cellophane from the deck and threw the double jokers into his hat and began to shuffle. No one watched the shuffle or the deal because they doubted The Shooter. They watched because as a group of professionals they appreciated the truly fine way in which The Shooter could handle a deck, forearms resting about halfway and tight against the edge of the table, his big hands dangling a scant few inches above the deck; the cards whirred, were alive and then melted in his huge paw. He shuffled six times, once each for the number of men at the table and slammed the deck down before The Kid. The Kid merely nodded and blinked his eyes to deal without a cut. It was the highest honor that could be paid a rambling-gambling man and The Shooter acknowledged this with a quick nod of his head, rapped the table lightly to signal the deal. With the deck cradled in his big broad palm, with the barest motion of his wrist, and more of a snapping movement of his fingers, The Shooter pitched the cards toward the players, each card landing exactly where he wanted it to land, coming to a stop six inches away from the players' money and yet clearly in view of everyone at the table. He repeated this movement without pausing a second time for the up-card round and it was almost impossible to see the difference in the motion of his hands as the cards were now pitched face up and showing.

"Trey, jack, nine, ace, trey and The Shooter guns up a queen. Ace bets."

The Kid had an ace in the hole to go with his trey. He watched the board. Lancey had the second ace.

"Ten dollars," Lancey said in his quiet way, smiling quickly and looking up at Carmody on his right.

Everyone stayed. The Kid caught a second trey on the third card and no one stayed. He pulled the pot. The Shooter shuffled again, dealt.

It was a repeat. Lancey opened for ten, everyone stayed and The Kid caught an open pair on the third card and everyone folded.

"New deck," Lancey said, brushing his fingers as he rippled the edge of his money. It was a request any of them could make at any time during the game, but no one would, allowing The Kid and Lancey to call for cards. The Shooter nodded, gathered in the cards and along with the jokers he had taken from the sealed deck, separated them into five piles and then ripped them with five quick pulls of his powerful fingers, turning and handing them to Corrigan who in turn went and flushed them down the toilet.

The Shooter broke open his second deck and repeated the process of taking out the jokers, shuffled six times and gave them to The Kid for a cut. This time there was a cut. Having once signified his confidence in the dealer, the cut was important since there was always the chance that someone would see the bottom card. A card known to be on the bottom of the deck could not be a man's hole card. It was important.

The Shooter gunned them out, laying them with the precision of a machine.

When The Kid saw Lancey play a hand that was not a no-stay hand, which is what everyone at the table was playing for an hour or more until they warmed up and began to feel the cards and had worn through the initial nervousness of the game, he saw why Lancey Hodges was The Man.

The Shooter had folded. Having neither a good hole card, or a good up-card, and therefore already having lost 40 per cent of his potential, with only three cards left to give him any power, he dropped out, no-stay. Then Carey did the same thing. The Kid dropped out on the third card. The Kid was sure Pig was holding a nothing with his pair of queens. Carmody was playing wild for a straight heart flush, since there was no other reason for his staying against the queens, and which he should not have done in a game with Lancey, and though there had only been one other heart to show, and at most two in the discards, it was still wild poker. And Lancey on the fourth card was showing three jacks. It was the last card.

"Check," Lancey said evenly, giving Pig and his two queens a quick impersonal smile. Pig nodded. He hesitated a moment. And the hesitation was like a cold wind, the kiss of death and The Kid saw it.

"Check," Pig said.

It was only a small thing, but The Kid noticed Lancey brushed his fingers. Carmody checked. The Kid smiled. Carmody was getting off light. The last card could have cost him money. For a moment The Kid wondered why Lancey had not taken the pot right then and there. A big bet would have chased both Carmody and Pig with his two queens. And then, even as he wondered, The Kid saw through Lancey's plan. He was going to try and throw a scare into The Kid by taking Pig over the coals. If Carmody didn't bomb in with the heart on the last card, in which case he would have it all, and which was very unlikely, Lancey was going to play it cute. The Kid suppressed a smile.

"Last card," The Shooter peeled the cards and laid them in perfectly, Carmody busted his flush. Neither Lancey nor Pig got help.

"Jacks bet two hundred," Lancey said, sweeping his hand out and dropping ten fluttering twenties into the middle of the table. There was already more than three hundred in the pot. Lancey settled back in his chair and studied his money, rippling the edge of his two-inch stack of tens.

Pig rocked back in his chair and folded his arms over his chest and studied the ceiling. Everyone in the room knew what he was doing. Pig recalled the hands and he was working the percentages. The Shooter had folded with a ten showing. If The Shooter had held a pair, or had help with a jack or better he might have bought a third card. The Kid had held a four, caught a seven and dropped. A jack could have been buried, but with Lancey holding an open pair, The Kid would have folded. The Kid was a question mark.

Then Pig came forward and looked at Lancey's cards. Three bold bustling jacks, stark, staring, two one-eyes and a two. Carey had caught a nine. He would have had to stay with a decent pair, and could have dropped even if he had a high card in the hole. He could have folded the fourth jack. Carmody had been working on a heart straight that would have run no higher than a ten.

Lancey had opened with a fifty-dollar bet and a jack showing and then caught a second and a third. Lancey had had the board beaten with his first jack and could be figured jack or better in the hole. The fifty-dollar bet was important.

The recall was in Pig's favor. Everyone knew this. Lancey knew it also. The Shooter exercised his right as dealer to call the game into action. "Two hunnert to the queens," he said tonelessly.

The trap closed in on Pig. He rippled his money. "And a hundred better," Pig said and they all saw his hand shake.

"That, and five hundred more," Lancey said

♠ 99

quietly, with no smile, coming back with a no-nonsense move of his hand, and dropped the bills into the middle of the table.

Pig swallowed hard. No one looked at him. They did not want to see his face. The Shooter knew he wasn't going to make the bet and did not press him. They all studied their money and lit a cigarette and waited for Pig to fold.

He swallowed once more and reached with a shaking hand for his hole card and flipped his two queens face down. Lancey dragged the pot.

Pig watched Lancey's hands hopefully for some sign of that hole card as the winner stacked his cards face down and slid them over to The Shooter who gathered the secret of the fourth jack into his huge fist and lost it forever in a quick shuffle and no one ever knew, nor would they ever know, if the fourth jack was there or not, but they would remember the hand a long time.

The cards ran to very good or very bad. The Kid bought several very good pots and The Shooter too, playing his steady game of conservative poker that was an investment at the narrowest possible margin of sure profit. It was very hard to play stud poker the way The Shooter was playing. Each card changed the odds and percentages of each hand, and with each change there had to be figured in the size of the bet and the size of the pot and the probable odds of the bets that would follow. To play the kind of poker The Shooter played, the rambling-gambling man had to have an IBM calculator for a brain and no nerves at all. Carmody, playing his game of plunge, brilliant at the fringes and fuzzy in the middle, which is what kept him from being in the top class, was up and down. Carey played like The Shooter, but with less luck and finesse, because there was no room in a game for two margin men and as a consequence, since The Shooter was getting the cards and because he was a better player, Carey lost steadily with his no-stay game.

Pig never recovered from the hand where Lancey had caught and chased him, and he began to bet recoupment with bad cards, trying to chase people out and couldn't and was not winning. Lancey bucked The Shooter three times, taking one good pot and one that was so-so, and The Shooter took a very good pot. The Kid and Lancey had not yet come to grips with each other. At midnight the game had shaken down with Carmody a big winner so far, The Shooter ahead and about where he expected to be with his narrow margin game that he played so steadily, never being tempted to come out of his shell and plunge unless he had them stacked up. Carey quit a loser after he saw that The Shooter was taking most of the conservative pots. Pig had dropped seven hundred. Of the eleven hundred dollars that had been lost by Carey and Pig, Lancey had two hundred and seventy-five, The Shooter, a hundred seventy-five, The Kid two hundred fifty, and Carmody had four hundred. The Kid took Pig's last hundred and twenty dollars using a full house with tens to take the pot away from Pig's full house with eights. The last hand, including the no-stay money and the drop outs brought The Kid up to an even five hundred winner.

"Break?" The Shooter asked.

The Kid looked at Lancey and protocol demanded that they yield to Pig, who was the loser. Pig stood up, his face was drained of color and his hands were shaking. Everyone pushed back and waited.

"Want to raise your roll?" The Shooter asked. "Half hour."

Pig bit his lip and hesitated. He scratched his cheek. "No," he said finally. "I'm out."

"You Tap City?" The Shooter asked.

Pig clenched his teeth. It was the worst moment for a rambling-gambling man to admit that he had no more money and by admitting that he was Tap City, was asking for a gratuity. Pig nodded and every man in the game took a ten and passed it over to The Shooter who handed it to Pig. This was eating and sleeping money. He could not gamble with it, could not re-enter the game and he would have to return the money before any of the players would gamble with him again.

Taking Tap City did three things to a rambling-gambling man. It forced him to admit that he had lost and had gone broke and in the talk after the game, his sources of supply would surely hear of it and action money would be hard to come by and they would think carefully before piecing him off with a roll. The second thing was the more important of the three. It took him out of action. And, finally, it snowed his confidence. Many did not recover.

Pig did not move. "I got a woman," he said.

The Shooter looked up, his face clouded over. "I thought you and Hilda were quits."

"We're back."

Everyone waited for The Shooter to make the decision and finally The Shooter turned to the table. It would have been death for Pig as a rambling-gambling man to lie about it. The Shooter nodded to the table and they all anteed up another ten. The Shooter handed the money to Pig. "See you around, Pig," he said easily, with a tone of dismissal that left nothing else to be said.

"Yeah," The Pig murmured, looking at the money in his hand. He stepped to the door and held the knob in his hand, then turned back and looked at Lancey who was rearranging his money. "Good luck, Kid," he said deliberately, and then he was out of the door.

Lancey jerked his head up and his pale gray eyes flashed. His lips tightened and he looked at The Shooter. But he didn't say anything. The reaction at the table to Pig's statement was a low brooding silence.

The Shooter cleared his throat and felt obligated to apologize to Lancey, since Pig was a local gambler and in the game strictly on The Shooter's recommendation. Lancey did not know Pig personally. "His woman," The Shooter said, "wants him to cut out and go square. She's got him by the balls."

"He shouldn't have said that," Lancey said in a clipped way and in a tone that was as cold as ice. "Not after taking Tap City from the table."

The Shooter was slow in answering. He took the time to light one of his huge cigars and puffed it several times. "Don't spread the word on him, Lancey," The Shooter said around the cigar. "You rattled him with that jack hand of yours."

"If Big Nig was here now," Lancey said, his voice still cold and not a little waspish, "he'd be finished from Pittsburgh to Vegas."

The Shooter had made two bids to ease Lancey's feelings at the breach of protocol. He clamped down on the cigar and kept his mouth shut.

It was up to The Kid now. The Cincinnati Kid looked up and across the table and level with Lancey's eyes. "I don't need his luck, Lancey," he said easily.

Lancey looked at The Kid a long time, their eyes level with each other's and he smiled his thin smile at The Kid at the far end of the table. "Okay by me, Kid," he said easily, and it was all gone.

104 ♠

Everyone relaxed. The Shooter stood. "Let's break and shake down," he said, knowing that it was early for a break, but not wanting any more tension in the game than was necessary. It was The Shooter's game and whatever happened with Lancey and The Kid, the word would go out that it was The Shooter's game. He wanted it to go out that it had been right between The Kid and Lancey, because it was his game.

As soon as they stopped the play, Corrigan was there with coffee. Old Lady Fingers came in and wanted to know what had happened to Pig.

Though it was the first break, and early, The Shooter let the crowd in to help get rid of the tension caused by Pig, and the crowd came in then, eager to hear about the game and to learn how Lancey had busted Pig wide open.

They came in, a little loud, full of enthusiasm, a few local gamblers and the big timers, Wildwood Jones, Miriam, Yeller, Shorty, Spriigi, Jolly, all of them a little high from their drinking, but nowhere close to being drunk. A few dicemen had stopped by to see the action. They were a prime source of supply to a card man on the edge of his stake and needing stake money. The presence of a police lieutenant put the official blessing on the proceedings, so there would be no fear of a raid. The lieutenant told everybody who would listen that this was not just an ordinary poker game but a championship match and deserved a certain respect. There was a famous restaurateur, a fair stud man himself, who had taken a two-room suite next door to 311 where he had food and drinks brought up from his restaurant. He delighted in fixing the brandy and coffee for The Kid, the crème de menthe frappé, and The Shooter's ice-cold bottles of Bud and declared himself the official host of the game. The Shooter's woman was there, walking tall through it all, searching her man's face for signs of strain and fatigue, pairing off with Carmody's woman, who was quiet and not at all worried about her man winning or losing since she was independently wealthy and Carmody was never at a loss for a stake.

A few purists were there, too, the lovers of the game, the squares who played in country clubs and had "poker nights" and never played more than quarter and a half, and weekend players who held square jobs during the week and supported wives and mothers and kids by fleecing their friends and neighbors in friendly little games. There were some young business types in their Ivy League clothes and crew cuts who were very sincere and talked low and spoke of percentages and odds as though they were reciting beads in church, and with them were their women who are all hawk and no spit and who are very serious and found it all culturally beguiling and sociologically interesting, who had never seen big-time gamblers before and who looked around bright-eyed and said very little even when they were talking with their mouths wide open. There was a famous golf pro who was notorious for his poker losses and who fancied himself a rambling-gambling man and liked to associate with them and who liked to make sure that everyone saw that The Shooter, or The Kid, or Lancey knew him by name. He told everyone who would listen that he felt he had made the wrong decision, and that he really belonged on the road with a few bucks and a deck of cards, a stud man, instead of one of the best golf pros in the business.

It was a long break considering the game had not been under way very long. The restaurateur, as self-appointed host, but with The Shooter's nodding approval, moved the crowd in and out of the small room with practiced, professional ease, jovial and firmly polite. He got the moochers and squares and the nobodies out by inviting them to his suite for a drink. The break shook down finally to just a handful.

A Hollywood director and a famous male star dropped in and their Hollywood women, both tall and willowy, looking at the local women and watching them and smirking at the pretense because the Hollywood women had been around and were in and not squares.

The Kid and Lancey, one after the other, excused themselves and went into the bathroom, and then stood and spoke to each other as the crowd stood in awe and tried to hear what they said. They were very conscious the two giants were speaking to each other in a friendly way and only the true professionals in the room knew that either one or both of the giants were killers, and had the sure instinct for the jugular vein, and that the friendly talk was not friendly but guardedly respectful.

"Good crowd," Lancey said.

"Yeah," The Kid said.

"Nice groceries, too."

"And good booze. My brandy must be Napoleon."

"Uh-huh."

"Yeah."

"Nice-looking broads."

"That's a fact," The Kid said.

"Ain't that Shooter something? Love to see him skin a deck."

"It's downright sexy," The Kid said.

"He loves 'em."

"Like stroking a beautiful tit," The Kid said.

"That's it — that's it," Lancey said, nodding.

"Yeah."

"You seen him yet?"

"No. You?"

"No."

"I dint hear he wasn't coming," The Kid said.

"He'll come, Kid," Lancey said, almost, but not quite, warmly and reassuringly.

"I sure hope so," The Kid said. "I like Nig."

"Well, I do *too*."

"I heard talk."

"Long time now."

"It ain't hard to like Nig."

"Not at all."

"Him sitting down yonder in Memphis and he knows it *all*."

"Everything."

"They oughta take him into the intelligence."

"They ought."

"Pig shouldn'ta done that."

"No," Lancey said. "He was wrong. Dead wrong."

"I ain't apologizing."

"I know it — I know it."

"It's just — "

"Kid, I know all about it," Lancey said.

"Yeah, you been around."

"Long time."

"Now, I ain't talking cards," The Kid said, "but Pig, well, he — no man can play cards with a woman got a hook in your balls."

"Don't — I — know — it!" Lancey said, smiling his quick smile.

"That's his whole case."

"Kid, I got his money, that's all that counts."

"Ain't it now. Ain't that the truth? As if I dint know it," The Kid chuckled.

Lancey turned and looked at The Kid and patted him on the arm. The Kid turned and looked at him and waited.

"Listen, now, I'm going to get myself some of them good eats that big fellow's spread out next door. You hungry?"

"You go on," The Kid said. "I don' eat much when I'm working."

"Take your time, Kid. I ain't in no hurry."

"Same to you, Lancey. Anytime you wanta break, an' all, why, take it. You know what I mean."

"Sure-sure," Lancey said. "Well, I'm going to see what the food is like. Lemme know when you're ready."

"We leave it to The Shooter? Okay?" The Kid said seriously. "Let The Gunner decide."

"Sure-sure."

Lancey turned away from The Kid and was stopped by two of the very serious young men who wanted to ask Lancey a lot of questions. The Kid could not hear what was asked, but he heard Lancey's polite reply.

"The difference between me and The Cincinnati Kid is so slight, you have to go all the way back to luck. We know it all."

They tried to ask him something else, but The Shooter stepped in quickly and queered it and Lancey escaped out the door.

The Shooter stood in one corner of the room with his woman and Hoban and the Hollywood crowd and talked, lighting up a two-dollar cigar, nodding his head as the director talked, and made an argument for himself to the big man. The Shooter was like a paternal giant, above it all, the elder statesman of the group, who had a permanent place among the rambling-gambling men and did not have to prove anything and therefore could deny the director a seat in the game.

"Shooter Man, let me in just to drop a little," the director pleaded. "I know I'm not in the same class with The Kid and Lancey, but they wouldn't mind picking up some loot."

"You gotta unnerstand, Yasha, this ain't amatoor night. This is Academy Awards," The Shooter said.

The Shooter's woman, who was very good at this sort of thing, moved in on the director with the ease and grace of a den mother putting the soak on a fist fight.

"I saw your last picture, Yasha."

At first when the crowd came in, and after they had looked at the trappings of the game, the tables and chairs, the money that was left on the table, the decks of fresh cards, they talked in low tones. But when Old Lady Fingers began to show off her way with cards which was good, but with tricks and fancy, and not as straight and classical as The Shooter's way with a deck, the crowd began to liven up and get loud as they replayed the hands, especially the jack hand that had rattled Pig. They talked about the absolutely terrible behavior of Pig and speculated on what would happen to him when Big Nig found out about it. At first they were impartial about who they were for, Lancey or The Cincinnati Kid, but when the crowd broke up into three groups, those around Lancey in the next room where the food was spread out, those around The Kid, and a smaller, older group around The Shooter, the tone changed and came out for The Kid.

The Kid had seen it all before. He stood to one side with the tight-faced, eager, pinched women who asked him a lot of stupid questions and smoked cigarettes one after the other and held one drink all during the break, their wrists slightly bent backward and away from the body as if they were about to offer it to someone. The Kid tried to answer their questions without being rude, and even as he did he was aware that he had seen it all before. But there was a difference. This time he was not a member of the crowd that came in to look during the break, but one of the men on the line.

About halfway through the break, when he was alone for a moment, he looked around and tried to catch The Shooter's eye and give him the signal he was ready to go again. He found him smoking a cigarette and looking down at the table where Lady Fingers was putting the finishing touches on a neat display, and not seeing The Shooter sighed and settled to wait.

"Doesn't this break do something to your concentration?"

The Kid puffed on his cigarette and looked up from beneath his eyebrows. The woman was tall and plain, but she knew all the tricks and how to dress and this made her something more than just pretty.

"It doesn't help any," The Kid said, looking her up and down.

"I shouldn't think so," she said.

"You play stud?"

She turned her head, once having caught his interest and attention, and blew smoke into the air and looked out over the room. "I'm not professional."

The Kid had seen her type before. The clothes, and the careful way and the casual, confident air that would be called arrogance in a man, but that was called coolness in a woman. Money. Boredom. Indulgent. Careless.

"My name is Marguerite della Vichia. I'm at the Washburn Hotel."

The Kid said nothing.

"Do you think you'll win?"

"If I get the cards," The Kid said.

"And you're The Cincinnati Kid."

He looked at her.

"Do you have a square name?" She smiled, her eyes boring in, but soft.

"Eric."

"Eric what?"

"Lady," The Kid said, dropping the cigarette to the carpet and grinding it out, "why do you want to know?"

She lowered her lids and looked away, out and over the room. He waited for an answer and then without looking at him again, she walked away and joined the group around The Shooter.

The Shooter had to refuse the director again as well as the golf pro, and they didn't argue about it since The Shooter was running the game and the object of the game was not profit, or amusement, but a duel between The Kid and Lancey.

There were still many others in the hall and around the door, smaller fry that could not get inside and into the room because the restaurateur kept them all out, but who looked in and oohhhed and aahhhed at the famous movie star and blinked at the beautiful women and gulped and wondered and listened to the stories, and then it was all over and The Shooter was calling a halt to the break and asking everyone if they would please leave.

The director and the golf pro made one last appeal to The Shooter to sit in and The Shooter refused, firmly, but softly, appealing to them to understand they were not in the same class with The Kid and Lancey, because The Shooter did not want to foul up any future sources for a roll if he should tap out and want to get back into action.

The golf pro went over to The Kid and to Lancey and shook hands and pointedly refrained from wishing either of them luck, but simply nodded and squeezed each man on the shoulder.

She was one of the last to leave. She looked at The Kid. "Washburn Hotel. Marguerite della Vichia."

Corrigan cleaned up the coffee cups and The Shooter waved a newspaper around to clean the smoke out of the room and finally the room was cleared and everyone settled back into their chairs and The Shooter picked up a fresh deck and the game resumed.

From then on the game was whispering silent and charged, and the play went rapidly. The Kid began to loosen up and show how far he had come and they all saw this and were secretly proud of him. He began to creep up on Lancey, stealing pots away from him with third and fourth card bets that were shrewd and masterful, never too much to chase Lancey, not enough to show over-confidence, forcing Lancey to bust and then dragging the pot.

Lancey was not the only one who was feeling the pressure The Cincinnati Kid was putting on. Carmody lost it all in three hours of play, a total of seventeen hundred dollars. He backed away from the table refusing Tap City because everyone knew that his woman had plenty. Everyone at the table was a little sorry to see Carmody break out because he had provoked excitement often in a game that was fast becoming a duel of pressure and psychology and that was so pure that the finesse of the playing was lost to all except The Shooter, Lady Fingers, Lancey and The Kid. The Shooter had gained a respectable share of the winnings with over twelve hundred and now, comfortable that he had asserted himself in the game with the big men, began to lay off, buying cards with no-stay, and only coming out when he had them wired.

With Lancey Hodges, The Cincinnati Kid tried no tricks. He felt the urgency of the game rising in him and looking at his stake and remembering the hands, he felt for the first time that he might have a chance. And Lancey was reacting. He could see the difference in Lancey's play and The Kid knew that Lancey was taking him seriously. And there was a change in the way The Shooter was calling the cards. The Kid had an absolutely perfect ear for such things. Win, lose or draw, he knew he would come out of the game with the respect of The Shooter and anyone else who was interested.

They ran through nineteen deals with one or both of them turning their cards over, no-stay, before they both caught hole cards and The Kid opened for a hundred. It was two-thirty. The Kid went in on the third card with a three-hundred-dollar bet and three aces. Lancey folded. He went in once more, five hands later, with a two hundred dollar bet and three tens and Lancey folded again.

The third time they locked horns, The Kid knew that Lancey had four kings and let himself be chased and dropped six hundred. But Lancey knew this too and so did The Shooter and the others, and it did not count. There was a long dry spell when they turned their cards over and played no-stay with either The Kid or Lancey opening for fifty or a hundred and the other one folding.

Then quickly in rapid succession they played honest stud poker for nearly ten hands in a row. They played it straight, no bluffing, no one chasing the other out, and they just played and bet the cards, a slow form of showdown poker, with very large bets and no real interest since there was no real argument about who had what. Out of this The Kid came on very strong and picked up nine hundred. He looked down at his money. He knew that there was about five thousand in his table stake. He was in good position now. He settled with the urgency and began to ease up and felt that it would not be very long now, and with his money, he could go in on any play and stand up to Lancey.

They were both getting tired now, both of them were making frequent trips to the bathroom and they both had taken to their drinks. The Kid sipped his brandy and coffee and Lancey sipped his crème de menthe frappé through a straw and then cracked the ice in his teeth. They had both removed their jackets and shoes and Lancey, who suffered from constipation, was sitting on a pillow.

The Shooter called a halt at seven. "I break," he said. "Sitting here dealing ain't like playing. No real incentive or interest, know what I mean, gents? I gotta eat and sleep. If you wanta go on playing, I'll call Lady Fingers."

"Well, I ain't sleepy," The Kid said. "But I am hungry." He looked up at Lancey for approval.

"I am too, Kid," Lancey said quickly. "Hungry, I mean. Suppose we take a break and see to some breakfast?"

"Good enough," The Kid said.

"Gents," The Shooter said with a formality in his voice that had characterized his behavior all the time of the game, "the food is on me. We can stretch our legs and go over to Victoria's, or we can stay here in the hotel, which has some very fine food."

"Would Victoria be open this early, Shooter?" Lancey asked.

"She told me she would be open anytime we needed anything for the game. Them was her words."

"Wouldn't there be a gang over there?" The Kid asked.

"That wouldn't bother me, Kid," Lancey said.

"Then let's get some air, Lancey, if you want to, I mean? If it's okay with you."

"Fine-fine, Kid. Sure-sure," Lancey said in his usual brisk way, smiling quickly.

"I'll call, get her to have things ready when we get there," The Shooter said, standing and stretching.

"Victoria has a place down to Arkansas that she gets special hams and bacon and sausage," The Kid said pleasantly. "And country fresh eggs."

"I like that," Lancey said. "There isn't anything like fresh eggs and sausage and milk after a night of working."

"I buy that," The Kid said.

"Uh-huh."

While they waited for The Shooter to make the call to Victoria, and while Corrigan and Old Lady Fingers were awakened and invited to come with them for breakfast, Lancey stood at the window looking down into the early morning busy street.

"I hate St. Louis in the summer," Lancey said to The Kid.

"Oh?"

"The heat."

"I don't mind it," The Kid said.

"Cincinnati, huh?" Lancey said.

"Born and raised." The Kid walked over to the second window and stood there, tall, skinny, a little humped over in the shoulders looking down into the street.

"I suppose you know I'm from the South. Savannah. Even so, I can't stand the heat," Lancey said.

The Kid remembered Miriam's description of Lancey, but said nothing. He listened politely as Lancey continued, learning a little more about this brittle little man who played poker with such control and ease and did not ruffle, and who looked so much like a banker or a small-town doctor.

"I like Miami. It's beautiful down there. And they have some beautiful hotels. Beautiful." Lancey turned and looked at The Kid. "You been down?"

"Not yet," The Kid replied. "But I heard a lot about it."

"Lovely," Lancey said. "Really. Ought to try it sometime, Kid. Lot of room down there."

The Kid nodded his head, in acknowledgment of the plain offer that Lancey would not ill consider it if The Kid moved into Miami and the big games that came with the season while Lancey had it staked off.

"I been thinking about Vegas — " The Kid said.

"Now that's nice," Lancey said. "Vegas."

"Uh-huh, I heard."

"A little wearing on the nerves, though. Can't ever get enough sleep in that town. So much going on. Action everywhere you turn. You lose the feel of the cards when you're in so much action day in, day out."

The Kid nodded.

"But the scenery is very calming. Big, great big flats — the desert you know — and mountains. Nights are cool. Wonderful floor shows."

"Is that a fact," The Kid said politely.

"Get all the big Hollywood stars there to entertain. I've seen them all, Danny Thomas, Judy Garland, Bob Hope, Sinatra."

"Sounds good."

"And like I say, lotta action. Anything you want."

"I'm a stud man," The Kid said, stating a fact.

"Well — I am *too*. But I like to lay off once in a while and try craps. Nothing serious — " Lancey said with a quick, fleeting smile.

"Oh, I do *that*," The Kid said. "But nothing serious. I shoot a little casino."

"Uh-huh."

"Yeah. And sometimes I get careless and buck some twenty-one."

"Uh-huh."

"I dint see Big Nig, did you?"

"No. But he could still come," Lancey said. "Which one was your woman — when we took the break last night?"

"None of them," The Kid said. "We just quit each other."

"Oh."

"Yeah."

"Too bad."

"She wanted it that way."

"I see," Lancey said softly, and then glancing sideways at The Kid. "You burning?"

"Me? Naw! But she was nice," The Kid said with a rare smile and a shrug of his shoulders. "How about yourself?"

"I don't look for a fixed thing any more. I just pick up a nice thing and when I'm away from the cards and the action, I enjoy it and — let it wear itself out."

"That's all right," The Kid said.

"It's a good way," Lancey said.

"Personally," The Kid said, "I always wanted a little more than just something to hold onto, and jazz a little, if you know what I mean."

Lancey looked at him, but did not speak.

"Like I had a little action once down to New Orleans, to Yeller's. There was this big pay off game on a ship — "

Lancey smiled knowingly. "I know them games. They're very nice games."

"So!" The Kid said. "I got to know this mate, that's one of the officers, and he had been a sailor a long time and all, and he told me when he went into a port he never hung around the waterfront with the other sailors, but got uptown, see, and met some woman and moved in with her for as long as he was there, with all the comforts of home and play the radio, come home after each day's work and all. It's like that with me, in a way."

"That's very interesting, Kid," Lancey said, watching The Kid, turned now, to face him.

"Well, that's the way things are."

"Sure-sure, I understand. Well, you're a lot younger than I am, Kid, don't forget that," Lancey said with a truly warm smile.

"A man can't change his nut."

"Nooo, a man can't do that."

"Things work out a certain way."

"They do."

"And you can't mess around with them."

"It is not healthy at all."

"I was hoping Christian would run with me, and wouldn't try to make a big deal out of it."

"Did she try?" Lancey asked after a pause, looking out of the window.

The Kid took a deep breath. "Yeah," he said, letting the air come out slowly. "She tried. But a man can't change his way, because the way I see it a man's lucky he's got something going for him that he can hold onto."

"That's very interesting."

"She dint understand how it was with me and — " The Kid stopped short and did not go on.

"Between us?" Lancey said warmly and very gently.

"There ain't," The Kid said clearly, "but a few people, I guess, that would understand."

"No, not many outside of all who knows us, me and you."

"Yeah, I figure."

"Kid," Lancey said, "you the best stud man I've seen in thirty-five years of action. You know that?"

"I figured I'm good, but — well, thank you, though, Lancey."

"And I'm glad we had this little talk, and all," Lancey said. "So then I know we can be friends regardless what happens and things come out."

124 ♠

"Okay," The Kid said. "I dint think you was coming in at me like a grudge match."

Lancey grinned. "No room for any kind of emotion in a fair game of stud." He jingled a few coins in his pocket and looked out of the window. "I learned that a long time ago, when I was a young guy cutting the deal now and then and making my way. I saw the Dempsey-Tunney fights. That Tunney. He never got mad one time. But Jack was mad all the time. Jack lost the fight, I think, because he was mad and Tunney wasn't."

"Fighters are famous for being cold about it," The Kid said. "That's why using their fists in a street fight is a felony. They're cold and know what to do. A regular person like you or me wouldn't have a chance."

The Kid noticed that Lancey had not once brushed his fingers since they had taken the break, or at any time since they had been talking. And then he wondered if there was some nervous habit to which he was addicted and that he was unaware of, and then he realized that he was presuming that Lancey Hodges was unaware of his brushing his fingers together. He did not think so, but then it wasn't for him to say. He would not take the habit seriously.

"Well, maybe I'll see you down in Miami, Kid," Lancey said, turning to see who had opened the door, and seeing Lady Fingers enter the room, her hair in a handkerchief, her eyes a little red and puffy, wearing a plain skirt and blouse. She went immediately to The Shooter's chair and sat down. Corrigan followed her in with fresh coffee and a double shot of brandy for The Kid and a fresh crème de menthe frappé for Lancey.

"Yeah," The Kid replied. "And maybe I'll see you in Vegas."

Lancey smiled. "Might work out that way."

"Fine," The Kid half nodded and smiled.

They both turned from the windows and returned to the table.

"Where's The Shooter?" Lancey asked Lady Fingers.

"Taking a shower in my room. He'll be right in, Lancey."

The Cincinnati Kid and Lancey Hodges each took a turn in the bathroom where they washed, and The Kid gave himself a quick shave, and then they both sat down at the table, sipping their drinks, and watched Old Lady Fingers pick up the old deck of cards The Shooter had left on the table. She rippled them, shuffled them and displayed her ease with the deck and both Lancey and The Kid knew she was good and appreciated watching her.

"You're still good, Fingers," Lancey said. "Not as good as the old days down to Hattiesburg, and Baton Rouge and New Orleans, but still good."

"Getting crippled up, Lancey," she said in a tired voice.

She played with the cards beautifully and both

The Kid and Lancey knew she was not showing off or bragging, but she was playing with the cards and nothing else.

"Yeah!" Lady Fingers said explosively. "There aren't many of the old gang left. Me and you, Shooter, Yeller, Miriam." She stopped. "Did you hear that Sam passed over to the other side?"

Lancey remained perfectly still. "No," he said, watching Old Lady Fingers. "No, I didn't know."

"Year ago or so," she said. "I just happen to be passing through, making a little money playing bridge with Countess von Frankenberg — "

"Is *she* still alive?" Lancey asked.

"And still losing," Lady Fingers said. She looked up at The Kid. "If you're ever on the edge and you're in New Orleans, ask Yeller to set up some bridge with The Countess."

"Thanks, I will," The Kid said.

"Kid," Lancey said, "there is hardly a rambling-gambling man in the country that hasn't played bridge with Countess von Frankenberg at one time or another to get off the edge. You never heard of her?"

"No."

"She is a true Countess," Lady Fingers said, "and she loves cards. She made friends with Yeller a long time ago and they been playing a regular Tuesday and Friday night game as long as I've been around." She looked at Lancey.

He nodded. "I was playing with her and Yeller

♠ 127

the night I asked Yeller to set it up with me and old Sam."

"Yeah?" Lady Fingers looked at Lancey. "Is that a fact?"

"I had heard what he did to The Shooter," Lancey said. "And that was when I asked Yeller to set it up for me."

The Kid looked at Lancey. Whistling Sam Magee had taken The Shooter, and Lancey had taken Whistling Sam. The Kid was surprised to learn that Lancey had been The Man so long. There was something about the gambler that made The Kid feel that it was not something he had had a very long time. He looked at Lancey. It was almost as if Lancey had deserted his square job and turned to cards late in life, yet he realized this could not be so and have Lancey take Whistling Sam Magee.

They talked a little more and then The Shooter came into the room, his hair still dripping wet from his shower and rubbing it hard with a towel.

They did not talk cards at all, or discuss the game as they caught a cab and went over to Victoria's. They had a big breakfast which made everybody sleepy, and then all went back to the Dorset Hotel and slept until two o'clock that afternoon.

With Old Lady Fingers dealing in The Shooter's chair, she intoned the words The Shooter, who was sleeping and taking a break until that evening, had used. "This is a game of five card stud poker, gents, and there is no limit. Who was last under the gun?"

"Me," The Kid said.

Lancey Hodges got the first card and the game was resumed.

"A trey and a seven," Lady Fingers said. "Seven bets."

"Fifty dollars," The Kid said, betting his seven, and Lancey turned his cards over, no-stay.

By eight o'clock that night the tension of the game began to flow out of the room and to the halls and the suite of rooms the restaurateur had taken, down to the hotel bar and to the Glassways and Victoria's. Something had to happen, the crowd kept saying, it couldn't go on much longer like this. They had said that at six and then again at seven and now at eight, with the crowds more subdued, they waited. There was good reason for their belief that it could not go on much longer. The Kid and Lancey had been butting heads since two o'clock and it had been a see-saw duel, with Lancey dragging a big pot and The Kid coming right back on the very next deal and taking it all back. They had only played three no-stay hands since they had resumed the game, and at eight o'clock they were exactly where they were when they had started. The Kid had about five thousand dollars before him, and though he had been down to eight hundred once and down to fifteen hundred twice, he was never better, and for that, neither was Lancey, and as the insiders, Yeller, Miriam, Jolly, Spriigi, Wildwood and a few others began to ease through the door, quietly, slipping in behind the players and standing as still as dead people so as not to distract either of them, they saw that something had to give.

At nine o'clock, The Shooter returned, fresh and ready to take over as the dealer. Lady Fingers, who had not even gone to the bathroom since the game had picked up again, was nearly exhausted.

"I break," she said with a gasp of relief that was clearly an expression of pain when she saw The Shooter.

"I don't want no break," The Kid said with irritation.

"Well, I don't either," Lancey said.

"Deal," The Kid said, without looking at The Shooter.

The big man slipped out of his jacket, rolled his sleeves past the elbow and picked up a new deck.

"Same deck's good enough," Lancey snapped, not looking at The Shooter or The Kid, but looking at his money.

"I want a new deck," The Kid said, his voice low and almost sullen.

"All right-all right — a new deck then. Jesus!" Lancey said under his breath.

"Deal," The Kid said.

"Comin' out," The Shooter said. "Down, the dirty hole."

He peeled the cards off. It was as if a window was opened and a breath of fresh air came into the room. Where they had only had three no-stay hands in six hours, they now played for nearly four hours and either it was no-stay or they folded on the third or fourth card.

During this time The Shooter asked every hour on the hour if they wanted a break. Neither man would admit that he wanted to stop. Both of them were red-eyed and hung over from fatigue. The Kid had taken off his shoes and socks, his shirt, and sat in a T shirt with his trousers open at the top. Lancey had removed his jacket, his tie, and opened his vest and unbuttoned his shirt down to his trousers which were open at the belt also. He had taken his shoes off, but not his socks. Jansen came in at midnight with one of his assistants and while Jansen worked on the neck and shoulders and arms of The Kid, the assistant worked on Lancey.

Again and again The Shooter peeled the cards and laid them in before the players and put the deck flat on the table, rested his elbows and called the cards. Again and again it was no-stay or a third card fold. Only once did it ever get to a fourth card and The Kid dragged a nice fourth card pot of six hundred.

At two-thirty, Lancey caught a low heart flush hand, eight high. The Kid had a pair of tens showing on the third card and he bet five hundred, thinking to steal the pot of two hundred fifty. Lancey raised him three hundred.

The Kid did not move. He closed his eyes a moment and then moved his hand as if he were going to call, and then went on past to the cup and the remains of his coffee and brandy. He sipped it, stared down at the seven and eight of hearts. Until then, the bets and the calls, checks and raises had been so automatic that this slight hesitation in his play brought the attention of those in the room up sharply. They were already quiet. Now they did not even breathe.

If he just called, there would be eighteen hundred and fifty in the pot. It was by far the largest third card pot in the entire length of the game.

A seven and an eight. Hearts. The queen he had in the hole was a heart. What would Lancey have in the hole? A kicker? Ace? King? With two cards showing no power, the best a kicker could do would give him three of a kind, and The Kid already had a strong pair.

A third heart? Going for a flush? He had seven and eight, The Kid thought, and he would have to have a six heart card in the hole, because Lancey would not come on so strong in the face of an open pair of tens that could be three of a kind, without a six heart card in the hole. Lancey could build no higher than a jack heart card for a straight flush.

Eighteen fifty in the pot. Lancey would not chase. He had the open pair and the good solid queen in the hole. Solid two ways. Solid in power and solid because it was one less heart for Lancey to snare to make the flush.

And if he got his flush, The Kid would need four tens or a full house with queens. The percentages were in his favor. He felt something icy move up and down his spine as he took another sip of the coffee and brandy and put the cup down very slowly and deliberately, not too showy, but enough so Lancey could see it if he were looking for signs, holding the rim of the bottom of the cup above the saucer long enough for there to be no mistake about his being nervous.

Eighteen fifty in the pot. Lancey would not chase. And he could get a straight, a small straight at that, or a flush, in which case The Kid would have to get a full house, or Lancey could win it all with a straight flush.

Eighteen fifty in the pot. Lancey would not chase.

"Tens," The Shooter said. "Three hundred to the tens."

He's going, The Kid said to himself, for a straight flush. And I've got him.

"I see the three," The Kid said. "And kick it two thousand."

He swept his hand down to his money and with-out taking his eyes away from Lancey's face, he picked up the stack of fifty-dollar bills and counted them off, dropping them to the table, emptying his hand. Thirty-three fifty-dollar bills covered the middle of the table.

"Sixteen fifty," The Shooter said.

The Kid picked up tens and repeated his move, dropping them to the table in a flutter. Thirty-five ten-dollar bills were laid in an even cover over the fifties.

"And three hundred," The Shooter said.

The Kid dropped three one-hundred-dollar bills into the middle of the small mound of bills.

"Two thou to the seven-eight," The Shooter said.

Lancey had not moved a muscle the entire time The Kid was making his bet. He sighed and leaned back when The Shooter broke the spell of the silence with his chant of the bet.

Lancey picked up his glass of crème de menthe that was now watered down and looking like Pernod before water has been added, and sipped the juice off, staring at the table, then slipped a piece of the ice in his mouth and cracked it with his teeth.

"Two thou," Lancey said in a strong firm voice that everyone could hear and that was perfectly controlled, revealing no quiver or sudden phlegm that fear or nervousness might produce.

Lancey cracked the ice in his teeth and it was the only sound in the room.

"Call," he said lightly, almost abruptly, as simply

as if he were asking for a match. He put twenty hundreds together in a neat stack, counting them off so that The Shooter and The Kid could see that he was doing this and put the stack on top of the spread of fifty- and ten-dollar bills.

The Shooter rapped the table lightly one time. The people in the room moved in a step closer to the table.

"Fourth card," The Shooter said, dropping his right hand to the deck and without touching any card except the top card, peeled them off and put them in.

"A queen to the tens," The Shooter said. "And another heart, a ten heart to the seven-eight."

There was a very audible sigh in the room when the ten turned up with the seven and eight. The Shooter had only to turn his head and the room was instantly silent.

"Still tens," The Shooter said.

"Tens are worth one thousand," The Kid said, not hesitating an instant after The Shooter had made the call, and feeling the coldness up and down his spine again, and fighting now to keep anyone from seeing the pounding in his chest. He wondered if he dare put his hand down and scratch his knee which was suddenly itching so badly it was driving him out of his mind. The itch became so violent that his right leg began to jerk convulsively, but he did not move and sat as he had been sitting, motionless, hands on either side of his money, just in back of his cards. The knee was jerking and twitching so steadily now as he waited for Lancey to make his play, that The Kid's heel was tapping the floor. He did not move. He did not grit his teeth. He reached over and picked up his coffee cup and drained it. He put it down slowly and evenly. There was no rattle. He then picked up a cigarette and took his time bringing up a match and he looked at his hands to see if they were shaking and they looked like something not a part of him, and underneath the table his leg continued to jerk.

It showed confidence, that one-thousand-dollar bet, and they all saw that it was the perfect one to make. One thousand dollars was not too much to chase Lancey away from the nearly seven-thousand-dollar pot and it was enough to show at the same time that he had Lancey by the tail and wanted him to stay and was making this hand the big hand.

There were no other hearts showing except those that Lancey had, the seven, the eight and the ten. Catching the ten heart card busted The Kid's go for four tens.

"The bet is one thousand to you, Lancey," The Shooter intoned.

Lancey snapped his eyes up and looked at The Shooter and The Kid caught the expression, which was icy cold; they softened instantly, as Lancey smiled at The Shooter, but The Kid had seen the hard brightness and he knew that Lancey was unsure.

"A thousand is a cheap enough ride," Lancey said,

his voice easing back into a friendly quality that had characterized his manner early in the game. He picked up his hundreds and counted off ten bills from the stack. "One thousand for the call," he said.

When Lancey called the bet, those standing around would not be held back. They crowded in on the table and were so close Lady Fingers and Miriam were almost touching the side of the table itself.

The Shooter rapped the table lightly. "Last card comin' out."

The players waited. The Shooter picked up each card, snapped it and put them into the slot.

"A nine to the seven-eight-ten heart hand and a possible straight flush," The Shooter said. He flipped the card over to The Kid, pitching it in perfectly. "And another queen and a pair with the tens."

He leaned over the edge of the table. "Queens bet."

The Kid stared at the seven, eight, nine and ten of hearts and did not believe that Lancey had a jack or a six in the hole. He knew that Lancey was going to bet strong and try and chase him with a bluff of the big bet. But The Kid did not believe there was a straight flush against him, and his full house of three queens over a pair of tens had a simple straight beaten. Lancey was going to try and chase him.

But he didn't want just a showdown. He wanted Lancey to turn over his cards and show how foolish he had been, trying to buck for a straight flush when he had been beaten from the third card on.

The Kid looked down at his money. There was not more than fifteen hundred dollars left.

"Queens," The Shooter said, "is the bettor."

The Kid nodded. He looked down once more and then up at Lancey, who was looking straight at The Kid. The Kid figured Lancey to have about five thousand dollars before him. He was going to be about four thousand dollars shy.

"I'm taking my half hour," The Kid said, "to raise my roll."

The Shooter nodded and looked at Lancey. "Leave the cards and the money on the table, gents. It is now three A.M. The game resumes at three-thirty when the queens bet."

Lancey had not stopped looking at The Kid the whole time The Shooter was speaking.

The Kid started to get up when Lancey spoke.

"I'll take your marker, Kid," he said evenly. "Make your bet."

The Kid hesitated. He looked at Lancey. "I can raise it," The Kid said.

Lancey smiled. "I know you can, Kid."

"As long as you know it."

"I know it."

"Queens bet —" The Kid said, and heard his voice come out strong, and he began to count out his money. "Fourteen hundred twenty dollars."

He dropped the money into the pot. Lancey nodded and then picked up his money. He counted out fourteen hundred twenty dollars and then continued with all he had before him, starting the count all over again and coming to a stop when he was cleaned out. "I see the bet and raise it forty-one hundred even, Kid."

The Kid froze. All he had to do was tap the table to acknowledge that he was calling the bet and it would be over.

Lancey waited. The Shooter waited. Miriam, Lady Fingers and Carey and Wildwood Jones; Yeller and Carmody and Corrigan and the restaurateur and as many as could get into the room, waited and watched The Cincinnati Kid as he stared at the seven, eight, nine, ten of hearts and he could not move his hand.

"Forty-one hundred to the queens," The Shooter said.

The Kid did not move. He stared at his own cards and then at the heart hand opposite him, and he did not move. It was his hand. He had played it exactly the way he wanted to and yet he was considering turning over a full house, queens over tens in the face of what he was convinced could only be a four flush.

"Forty-one hundred to the queens," The Shooter said again. "Kid?"

He was not at all concerned about the mark of forty-one hundred. He had owed more than that, and he was not worried.

"You going to call, Kid?" The Shooter asked, and his voice was firm and businesslike.

The Kid rapped the table once, sharply. "Call," he said.

Lancey turned over his hole card and The Kid stared into the red face of a jack heart, and he did not realize for a moment that he had lost.

"That's forty-one hundred you owe me, Kid," Lancey said easily, with a quick smile, as he pulled the pot.

No one moved, or breathed, or looked or said anything and the only movement in the room was Lancey as he stacked his money. When he was finished, and when all of the fives and tens and twenties and fifties and hundreds were stacked, he turned to The Shooter.

"New deck," he said.

"You playing, Kid?" The Shooter asked. "You got one half hour to raise your roll."

"No," The Kid said quietly. "I'm tapped out."

The Shooter stood. "This game," he announced formally, "is over."

After Lancey had settled up with Lady Fingers for dealing the game, and had settled up with The Shooter for the hotel room and all of the expenses, while The Kid was in the bathroom getting himself cleaned up, he came out and he and Lancey shook hands like gentlemen and made small talk about the game, and how tired they both were and what a good game it was, the room was cleared out and Lancey said good-by, leaving with the police captain and several of the others.

The Shooter said later, after they had gotten The Kid so drunk that he passed out and they put him to bed, that he had gone to pieces. He also told Big Nig in a little note with his payoff bet, that he had never seen Lancey better. When he got hold of it, he never let go.

The Kid slept the clock around and when he woke up he refused to eat anything and turned to the bottle. The Kid and The Shooter got drunk and stayed drunk for five days and went over the poker hands and The Shooter reminded him that he had said The Kid wasn't ready.

The Kid accepted this and said very little.

When both The Kid and The Shooter ran out of money and ran out of their taste for Scotch, The Shooter and his woman sent a telegram to Christian, who came up the next day, with The Shooter and his woman waiting around for her, and then after they had turned The Kid over to her, taking the overnight down to New Orleans.

The Cincinnati Kid stood with his back to the street and watched the river gulls fish in the slate-gray Mississippi. The birds lazed aloft in long sailing glides and when prey was spotted they would cut loose and come in with their feet tucked up tight against their bellies. Sometimes the fish would dive and the river gull would pull up sharply. But this did not happen often. Then riding the water, they would throw their necks back and swallow the fish. Sometimes they would rest for long periods of time, but mostly they flew, gained altitude and started their hunt all over again.

He looked down at his hands. They were brown and did not shake any more. The noise of Harold Street and Broom Street did not bother him. He was all alone within himself and he was conscious that he had not had a drink in three weeks. He had gained a little weight and he knew that he was out of it and that he was all right again.

He swelled his chest and enjoyed the feeling of good health. At a warning footfall behind him, he turned and saw Pig approaching him. Pig had gone square after being gutted by Lancey and had not touched a card since. He had been very apologetic to The Kid and to Lancey, who accepted his apology, for his behavior during the big game, and though The Kid had reassured him a dozen times that Pig had nothing whatsoever to do with his losing, Pig still felt guilty.

"Hello, Kid," Pig said easily. "You feel better, eh? You sure as hell look better. You look like maybe you might even live. How long you been without a drink now?"

"Three weeks," The Kid said, tossing a stone into the river.

"Pretty good. Pretty damn good, you ask me. But it could be rough. I know. A man don't have to start out in life being a lush, but the way you been drinking since the game —! Man! My old man, who was a lush, said if a man could stay away from the booze for two weeks, he had it made. I used to watch my old man sweat it out. He never made it. I used to sit and watch him. He would paralyze himself for ten, eleven, twelve days and then fall off. He never did make two weeks. It was like he conned himself, you know, Kid? If he hadn't done that, set up two weeks as a mark, he mighta made the scene. The day he died, he looked up at me and said, 'By God, Oswald, I'm gunna make two weeks this time.' And he died."

All the while Pig talked, The Kid watched the river gulls work for their supper. "Sounds like a good man," The Kid said.

"My Pop? The greatest. But what are you going to do? A man's nut is his nut. You know. Booze. Wimmen, and so on."

"Or cards."

"Yeah, or cards," Pig said. "How's Christian?"

"Okay." The Kid threw another stone into the river and upset the catch of a gull who either had to miss his fish or dodge the stone. The Kid watched that one gull and saw that he made another catch almost immediately afterward and did not feel so bad about it.

"When you going to get back into action, Kid?" Pig asked.

"Maybe never," The Kid said slowly.

"You are kidding me," Pig said. "Not a pistol like you, kid. You couldn't give it up."

"I can. I think I have. Haven't I been living off Christian for three months now?"

"Look, there's a difference between a stud man like me and one like you. I can give it up easy. 'Cause I ain't got the call for it. It was just a way of getting by for me."

♠ 145

"It wasn't like that for me," The Kid said.

"I know it. That's what I mean."

"Well, then you know it all."

"The Shooter's in town."

"Oh?" The Kid said, interested. "How is he?"

"Well off the edge. He had a good summer down to Noorlins. Busted Yeller's wide open. He's down to Hoban's right now."

Pig watched The Kid's face carefully. "Why don't you come on down with me and say hello."

The Kid threw another stone in the river. "I'd like to, but I've got to meet Christian. If I don't show up at the place, she might think I'm drinking again and start worrying."

"Well, I just thought I'd tell you," Pig said.

"Thanks, Pig," The Kid said, looking at him. "If you see The Shooter tell him hello for me."

"Sure, I'll do that, but it ain't like your going down yourself."

"I know. But The Shooter will understand," The Kid said and threw one last stone into the river. "I got to go now and meet Christian."

"Well, so long, Kid," Pig said.

"So long, Pig."

The Kid walked off and stepped into Harold Street and went straight up to the coffee shop on the corner. He hung around the newsstand reading the headlines until the man handed him a day old *Sporting News* and The Kid read the box scores of how the Cards were doing and saw that Musial was hitting and being only six games out of the money, the Cards could still do it, if the Giants and the Dodgers folded, which was not very likely.

Christian came out then, taking him by the arm, a smile on her face, and he gave the paper back to the dealer, thanking him, and they walked back to their place which was one room.

"I made nearly eleven dollars today in tips," Christian said. "What would you like to eat tonight? Want to eat Chinese and take it up to the room?"

"No. I ain't very hungry," The Kid said.

"Well, you know how I am," Christian said, making a slight face. "I nibble all day on things and I would just as soon not eat. Want to go to a show?"

"No," The Kid said.

They walked on clear to their place without speaking again and The Kid knew what was on her mind and she knew that he was wary of her.

"I don't want to drink either," The Kid said. "So you can discard that from your mind."

"All right, Kid," she said.

They climbed to the room that was in the back and near a vent shaft over a café on the next street and that flooded their room with cooking odors. He took a cup of coffee and sat down in the big red stuffed chair overlooking Harold Street and stared out the window.

"The Shooter is in town," he said.

"Oh? Did you see him?"

"No. Pig told me."

"Why don't you go see him, Kid?" she said easily. "I can — take a bath and sit around and —"

"Maybe I will," The Kid said. "But he's down to Hoban's."

"Do you want to play?"

"I don't know," The Kid said.

"Kid, if you sit around waiting to be ready to go back to it, you'll never be ready." Christian said.

"I know that," he said.

"You haven't touched a card since the game."

"That's true."

"You going to sit around all this time?"

"How long is all this time, Christian?"

"Long enough to know — for me to know — that you stopped drinking, not because you knew it worried me, or bothered me, Kid, but because you were ready to stop and the hurt was burned out."

"Maybe I will go down and see The Shooter," he said.

"Kid, I wish you would. Get into some fifteen-cent stuff and start coming back, to me, will you please? I been away from you so long. I been away from you like you been away from cards, ever since the game. We got to pick up the pieces and go on, Kid."

He nodded his head quickly. "I see that," he said shortly. "But seeing it and thinking it and doing it, is two entirely different things. I dint start drinking 'cause I was carved up, and I didn't stop 'cause I was bleeding too much. Lancey ain't that kind of a man to do that to The Cincinnati Kid."

"Well, Kid," she said. "If you know it or not, that's the way things are. You carved up on the inside and Lancey's out there living — out there in the world — and you sitting here holding your hurts."

"I'm sorry." The Kid said stubbornly. "But I dint ask you to come up here and nurse me."

"Well what do you think I would do? Sit down yonder to the hills and let my whole life roll out from underneath me and not do anything about it?"

The Kid stood and looked at her. "I can take him, Christian. I know I can. Godammit! I should have known he had that heart jack! I should have known. He sucked me in like a baby just weaned — "

She looked up at him, nearly stunned by the ferocity of his words, and by the fact that he had spoken about it at all. It was the first time.

She went to her purse and came back to the side of the chair. She gave him a handful of bills.

"Go now. I don't care how much you lose, or anything about it at all. If that's what it takes, then I'll be your source of supply when you're on the edge." She thrust the bills in his hand. "You're The Cincinnati Kid, and don't you forget that that *means* something!"

They were silent, looking at each other.

"I'll be here waiting," she said. She reached up

and touched his face. "You're about to lose those yellowish circles under your eyes. A little more sun sitting out in the section at the ball park and you'll look wonderful."

He did not go directly to Hoban's. He could not. He wouldn't want to go and sit there and make a fool of himself and throw his money down the drain. He stopped off at the river and watched the last of the river gulls dive for their catch and he hung around until the river lights came on.

He decided he would go, but he would not play unless he felt it was right, but as soon as he bought a chair from Hoban and sat down, smiling sheepishly at the effusive greetings of the players, he knew that he wanted to play.

He came on strong and in three days, it was as if he had never been away. His feel for cards returned to him as if in answer to a prayer. Some big-time money and big-time players drifted into the game during the course of those three days, some of whom were not above sitting down with The Cincinnati Kid, hoping to knock him off quick so they could talk about it. But it didn't work that way. In those three days of card playing he made enough to pay off the forty-one-hundred mark he owed to Lancey and there was thirty-eight hundred over that. After he slept, he took a plane with Christian and The Shooter and his woman to Delray Beach where Lancey was just beginning to start his play on the winter circuit.

They played again, in a hotel room, with the millionaire crowd, the railroad and the airlines and the steel and the Wall Street crowd watching, and with them looking on, he lost again.

The way things are, they stop by and see how he is doing and maybe bull with him about the Cardinals and the Reds and ask his woman on the sly if he is okay and if he needs anything. They are very careful of his health and his feelings because they know that no man could take a beating twice and not have it affect him.

The Shooter stopped by more often than the others, but Pig and Carey and Carmody and Shorty and Corrigan and Wildwood Jones saw him too. Big Nig came up from Memphis on business and stopped off to see The Kid and stayed all night talking and talking. And Old Lady Fingers dropped in on her way East to try her luck with the winter cruise ships and get away from St. Louis's cold weather. They all asked him the same question, each in his own fashion: when was he going to quit the square job he was working at and get back into action.

When The Cincinnati Kid is very tired and he cannot sleep any more, he sits down in the red stuffed chair near the window overlooking Harold Street and Broom Street and stares into space that is filled with the noise of the kids and the pushcart people and the lasting noises of St. Louis preparing for the winter. His woman comes in and tries to help him, and put it in such a way that The Kid will understand that for every number one man there is a number two man, and that because of this, a man cannot retreat from life. The difference, his woman tries to tell him, is that the number one man is a machine and The Cincinnati Kid is not, and was not, and never will be a machine.

The Kid listens and never says anything as he waits for the urge to get up and go out into the world and be a rambling-gambling man, a three river man, again, and live with the truth about Lancey.

When the crisp nights come, his woman sits in the window and sings mountain songs, a soft knowing smile on her face as she waits with him.

Appendix

STRAIGHT FLUSH: Five cards of the same suit and in sequence. The ace, king, queen, jack, ten are a "Royal Flush." The ace may also rank low in sequence 5-4-3-2-ace.

FOUR-OF-A-KIND: As, in all four 7's, and any fifth card. (7-7-7-7-5)

FULL HOUSE: Three of one kind and two of another. (ace-ace-ace-king-king)

FLUSH: Five cards of the same suit. (As in ace-7-5-3-2 spades)

STRAIGHT: Five cards in sequence, but of two or more suits. (As in ace-king of spades, queen of clubs, jack of diamonds and ten of hearts) The ace ranks high or low, as in a Straight Flush.

THREE-OF-A-KIND: As, three aces, and any two other cards. (ace-ace-ace-5-8)

TWO PAIR: As, ace-ace-4-4, and any fifth card.

ONE PAIR: As, two aces and any three other cards. (ace-ace-4-8-9)

In Straight Flushes, Flushes, Straights and No Pair, the highest card wins. If the cards are identical in rank, then the next highest card wins, etc.

Four-of-a-Kind, or Three-of-a-Kind, the hand composed of the higher ranking cards wins.

Full House, the higher of the Three-of-a-Kind wins.

Two Pair, the highest pair wins. (If they are identical, then the highest of the second pair wins) If hands are equal, then the highest of the unmatched, or fifth card, wins.

One Pair, the higher pair wins; If these are identical, the highest of the unmatched cards.

If two hands are identical, they tie.

There are 2,598,960 possible poker hands.

Odds:

Straight Flushes	40	Three-of-a-Kind	54912
Four-of-a-Kind	624	Two Pair	123552
Full House	3744	Pair	1098240
Flushes	5108	No Pair, or better	1302540
Straights	10200